IMMORTAL DARKNESS

VAMPIRE MATES

USA TODAY BESTSELLING AUTHOR

LISA MANIFOLD

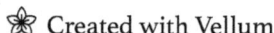

IMMORTAL DARKNESS

True love lives in the dark

When I walked into the darkened bar, I had no intentions of taking someone home - well, not for more than the night.

Then he walked in, and my vampire heart took a beat for the first time in more than a century. It's a sign - *the* sign, in fact. The one I never thought I'd get. He's my mate.

Chase is perfect - except for one thing. He's a third-generation hunter whose sole purpose on this earth is to destroy my kind. Does love truly conquer all? We're about to find out.

Lochdon House
Isle of Mull, Scotland

Angus–Kyla's mate
Charlotte–Talbot's mate
Clara–Lyall's mate
Collum -Isabeau's mate
Devon–Margaret's mate
Isabeau - Collum's mate
Kyla–Angus' mate
Lyall–Clara's mate
Margaret–Devon's mate
Morag–not mated
Talbot–Charlotte's mate

CHAPTER ONE

Morag

I watched my coven mates, arms crossed over my chest. All of them were in full lovey dovey mode. Even Collum, the head of our clan. He'd recently found Isabeau, and while it hadn't been planned, he'd turned her. Now they were together, and while I was happy for him, a small part of my heart ached for me. I wouldn't admit it to anyone else, but there was a small ache.

I'd been a vampire for over one hundred years. In all that time, I'd never found anyone who made my quieted heart beat once more. Fifty years ago, I'd spent time prowling the city streets, looking for someone who would ring my bell, give me a heartbeat, show me the way. Given that I lived with a lot of vampires who were mated, I felt the pressure. I wanted that for myself.

It hadn't happened.

So now, I just found men to bed. It was satisfying, and there were no strings. In fact, I decided that with all the love in the air, it would be a great time for me to take a weekend for myself and leave the rest of my coven to manage things here.

Collum felt my change of mood. He'd always been the one who had been most attuned to me. Even after mating with Isabeau, he was still the first one to sense my thoughts.

"What is it, Morag?" he asked.

"I think I'm taking a weekend off. Not like any of you plan to leave the house. And with all ten of you here, there's no one foolish enough to take you on," I grinned. Recently, there'd been a vampire stalking our house. He'd been after Collum, and he hadn't succeeded—but it was still enough to make everyone more watchful. If I left, there were still ten fully capable vampires to keep things going. There were benefits to being part of a larger coven.

Collum laughed, something that he did now with a regularity that Isabeau had come into his life. I liked the change in him, and I liked her. Her family had come to visit, and everyone but Collum and I had left. No one wanted to overwhelm Isabeau's family, or create any concern. We presented ourselves as brother and sister, both deathly allergic to the sun.

"Good thing you live in Scotland," Isabeau's grandmother had said.

Once Isabeau told them she was handfast with Collum, which was how they were presenting their mating to the world, and had no desire to leave, her grandmother sighed and told Collum and me to call her Gran. I couldn't remember my real grandmother, and the feeling of her patting my arm brought a warmth over me I hadn't expected. None of the rest of us had any family living. It was a gratifying experience, knowing there were humans out there who liked us. All in all, I felt that Isabeau was a good addition to our clan.

But that still left me, all on my own.

Clara nodded at me, understanding, as did Kyla. No one else made any comment, and later that night, after a bracing run in the woods, I made plans to go into Edinburgh. There was enough diversity there I'd be able to find someone to spend the night with and feed. All while flying under the radar.

I raced into Edinburgh on Thursday evening, making for the club district after checking into a hotel that I'd been staying at for years. It had a walk-in closet that kept the light out. What more could a traveling vamp ask for? I smiled to myself. I had some time before dawning and I was restless and wanted to dance and maybe feed before I went to ground for the day. I preferred Old Town and Candlemaker Row for student pubs. Tonight it was Cabaret Voltaire. It was small, dark, and old. Perfect for hunting for sex, or food, or both. While I was over one hundred, I didn't look more than my early twenties, when I'd been turned. College pubs were perfect.

The bouncers knew me by sight, so I breezed through the front, not waiting in line. The vibe tonight was delicious. There was an air of searching, of wanting—my favorite kinds of nights. I went straight to the bar and got a glass of red wine. I wouldn't drink it, but these evenings went better if I had a glass of something in my hand. While I waited on my drink, I surveyed the bar. Lots of men here. The women would come later.

Most were young, and out with their friends, having a good time. That wasn't what I sought tonight. There is actually such a thing as *too* shallow.

I looked around, not seeing anyone who—wait. I stared at the entrance. The hair on the back of my neck stood on end.

The light from the outside of the doorway framed a man. Tall, dark, emanating danger.

"Yes, please," I purred, pushing myself off the bar. As I walked through the room, he stood still for a moment, surveying everything going on around him.

He had the stance of a predator. There was a shadow around him that hinted of darkness and secrets. His hair and eyes looked dark, but that could be the lack of light in the bar. It didn't matter. He had an air of dangerous things around him.

Which was just what I liked. I slid around the people so I could get closer and watch him, wine glass in hand, not ready to let him see me yet.

His head turned toward me, almost as though he knew I was there.

I could feel strong emotion rising off of him. To look at him, he didn't look to be the emotional type. But it was there, and he was in some level of torment. Exactly my type. I may not want any strings, or anything permanent, but I liked those who were interesting. Who had a story.

Just to be sure, I took a lap around the bar, looking over any of the other prospects. I wanted to be certain this was the one for the night.

He was. Oh, he definitely was. The same emotion and danger I'd sensed in him when I saw him was still all around him.

Perfect. I moved toward him.

CHAPTER TWO

Chase

I scanned the bar as I came in. Always be alert. *You never know where they might be trying to hide, trying to pass.* My father's words rang in my ears. Lots of things rang in my ears now—the screams of the women, and the children.

The children. I'd never seen kids on a raid before. Never. My parents, however, didn't look surprised, and didn't miss a beat. The other Hunters we'd met up with for this raid—they were positively gleeful about it.

I'd been a Hunter for as long as I could remember. Even memories of early childhood were helping my parents get ready for raids.

"We're doing good work," my mom would say earnestly. "We're keeping the world safe."

"But why can't we tell people what we're doing?" I asked.

"Because people wouldn't understand. And it would scare them," she said. "We work for the knowledge that what we do keeps helps others. That has to be enough."

I'd believed that for most of my life. That we were doing good work, the work that had to be done. Work that we'd never get any credit for, that we couldn't even tell anyone about—but it was a good thing, and we would find reward at some point. The reward wasn't ever detailed, but my mother and father had been sure it was ours for the taking in the future. And I'd bought the whole damn thing. Until I was a teenager, and questioned everything, and wanted to go out, and have friends, and do normal things. But gradually, my rebellion faded, and I worked with my family, even as I wasn't as dedicated as the rest of them.

I'd thought there was something wrong with me, that I was the one lacking. That I was wrong for not being all gung ho. Until now.

Now, everything was different. I didn't know how I could go back, how I could pretend that everything was the same, that everything was still okay.

Because it wasn't.

The scenes of last night's raid ran through my head, making me wince. It wasn't a raid—I had to start thinking of what happened last night as what it was. It was torture. It was horror come to life. It was a massacre. And the kids... It was all *wrong*.

The images in my head were so fresh, so painful, that for a moment, I forgot where I was. Then the music changed, waking me from my reverie. At the same time, the bouncer leaned over toward me. "In or out, buddy."

I stepped in and caught a sense of—something. I turned my head, looking for the source. It was hard to tell what the something might be in this darkened bar, with all the bodies moving.

That was why I was here. I wanted to forget. Forget who I was, what we had done, what I was a part of. Forcing my instinct to shut off wouldn't work. But maybe I could silence it for one night. Just one. I ignored the voices in my head that screamed, *'All it takes is a minute. Let your guard down, and you're dead. Or one of us is dead. And it's your fault.'*

"Shut up," I muttered to the voices in my head that wouldn't be quiet. I needed a break.

I walked down the steps slowly to the bar and dance floor, still seeking the whatever it was I'd felt a moment ago. There were a lot of somethings in here, and I told my brain to stop. To shut off my Hunter.

Because tonight, I wasn't that man. Tonight, I was just Chase Robson, a guy in search of a good time.

Whatever the hell that was. I couldn't remember the last time I had a good time. My life was seeking out the undead and giving them the final death. It was all I'd ever known. And until tonight, despite my doubts, I thought this was the way life was. Doing something hard for the betterment of all. Even if I wasn't as all in to the idea of being a Hunter as I'd been as a kid.

Last night had showed me that my entire life was a lie. One, big, fucking lie. Tonight, all I wanted was to forget. Forget what had happened, what I saw.

Forget everything I was.

Forgetting might involve a woman, and there weren't that many here tonight. That was all right. I was flexible. Forgetting could be focused around too much to drink. That would work just as well, although it might not be as pleasant.

Then again, perhaps I wasn't fit for the company of anyone else, much less a woman. I mulled this over as I walked further in, feeling the shame and disgust come roaring back after everything that had happened in the past twenty-four hours.

The phone in my pocket buzzed. I'd been ignoring it since I decided to leave and come here—I pulled it out to look at it. Twenty-three missed calls. Dad, Brayden, and Cole. Most were from my dad.

"Piss off," I muttered, and I turned the phone off. I already knew what they were going to say, and I didn't give a fuck about hearing it.

I stopped again as I put my phone away. The tickle of someone, or something followed me in. I wasn't sure I'd be able to ignore that. However, I'd try.

As I headed for the bar, I felt an arm slide around my neck, the hand cool on my skin in contrast to the smoky warmth of the bar. Thankfully, it was my neck, and not my back or my waist. I'd hate to cry out in the middle of a place like this.

"Hello, there," a voice purred in my ear.

CHAPTER THREE

Morag

I carefully wrapped an arm around his neck, loving the fact that I had to go onto my toes to reach it. He was tall, and his hair was dark, sticking up in that messy way men wore it now. He had an air of desperation about him—not general desperation, but of a man lost from his moorings, looking for something more.

Well, for tonight, I could be that something more. This was a man on the edge. Just my type. Nothing permanent, nothing messy. I could feel the intensity in him vibrating like a drum.

"Hello, there," I said into his ear. I was glad I'd abandoned the wine glass on a table on my way over to him. I needed both hands for this. Sliding my other hand around, I let it rest on his chest.

He turned his head toward mine so that our lips were nearly touching. I could feel the heat of his breath, and the pounding of his heart.

"I'm not sure I'm in the mood for this," he said. His voice was rusty and broken.

"Oh, darling, I think we both know that's not true," I said.

"Listen, lady, you're— "he began.

"Just what you need," I sidled around to the front of him, putting both hands on his chest. "I can tell these things."

He looked at me, and in the darkness of the club, with people in motion all around us, everything stilled.

And then my heart beat. First once, as though it wasn't sure of how to still do it. Then again, a little faster. A third, then a fourth beat, and then my heart began to move as though it hadn't been stopped for over a century.

I looked up at him, my mouth open, my poise shaken. My heart was beating. Because of this man. I was so shocked that my heart was pounding that I didn't sense the change in him. Despite his earlier denial, he'd obviously made a decision. His arm snaked around my waist and pulled me to him. He kissed me, his lips hard and demanding, and below that, the desperation I'd felt when I first saw him.

I wrapped both arms around his neck, still in shock that my heart was beating. There it was, beating in time with his. I could feel him, like I'd never felt another human before.

Jesus, Mary, and Joseph on the cross. My. Heart. Was. Beating.

"Dance with me," he murmured against my lips.

I nodded, letting him guide me onto the dance floor. I kept my arms around him, and he punctuated his movement with small kisses on my lips. When he lingered, I gently bit at his, making sure not to use my fangs.

That would completely kill the moment, and it wasn't time for that. Not yet, anyway.

He put his hands on my hips, keeping me close to him. We moved together in time with the music, locked in a world where it was the two of us, where everyone else seemed far away, even though I could hear the music and chatter all around us. His body close to mine, our hips moved together, and I felt the desire for him turn from a small flame to a fire. He moved as one who used his body regularly, who was physical and good at whatever it was he did. This was a man who knew his body well. Oh, this was going to be *fun*.

And my heart was beating.

The darkness he'd brought with him swirled around us both. I felt a heat rush through me, the desire to see him naked, to feel his body next to mine in every way possible. My fangs dropped down, and as I looked down to make sure he didn't see them, I took a breath to calm myself.

It was hard, because I could feel that he was on the same path I was—oblivion. To forget. To lose yourself. What would it be like to lose yourself in your mate? The thought made me dizzy. As I listened, his heartbeat was steadily increasing as his desire grew.

But as much as I wanted him, I needed time. I needed to make sure this was real. If this was my mate, the one fate had chosen—I wanted to be with him here, in the dark, to see if it lasted.

To see if my heart kept beating.

The music sped up, but we were twined together, dancing, kissing, and I found that I kept staring at him. This was my mate. My *mate*. After all this time, when I'd given up on the whole idea—and here he was.

"Who are you?" He whispered against my lips. "Where did you come from?"

I didn't know what to say. For the first time in decades, I had nothing ready in response. I gazed up at his eyes, wanting to get lost in them.

"Who are you?" He asked again.

"I'm the person you're looking for," I whispered. "You know it."

"I don't know what I'm looking for," he whispered back. I could hear the break in his voice.

"Then let me help you." I kissed him again, feeling our hearts beat together as I leaned into him. "You don't have to make that decision."

He didn't answer, but kissed me back. Flames of

desire licked at my body, making me hungry for him. All of him. His body. His blood.

His heart.

"All right," he said. "All right."

I wasn't sure that he even knew what he was agreeing to. I'd seen people after a war, after bombs went off close to them. They were shell-shocked, not completely aware.

That's what this man—my mate—reminded me off. He was shell-shocked by something. The question was, What? And how much baggage would that be? I might be over one hundred years old, but I was up on the modern idea of baggage.

My mate had it. An entire cart of baggage, no doubt. I didn't mind. Being a vampire was fantastic, and I wouldn't be anything else. But it came with baggage. I didn't hold that against him.

As if I would. Particularly my mate.

"Who are you?" he whispered.

"Morag," I said.

"Chase," he replied. "Chase Robson."

He was Scottish, if I was reading his accent correctly.

His arms tightened on me, keeping me close. I liked it. I was used to being the most dangerous thing in the room, and while I thought I still was, Chase had that sense of danger that made me think he could give me a run for my money.

There was a lot I liked about this man. I wondered if

that was the mating bond, or if fate had merely chosen someone who fit well with me.

"You want to get out of here?" I reached up to pull his head down to me, whispering into his ear as I bit down on the edge of it, again being careful to keep my fangs hidden. It was tough when I was this aroused but it was even harder because this was my mate.

I kept saying those words to myself. My mate. My mate. My mate.

After all these years! I couldn't wait to get him alone.

CHAPTER FOUR

Chase

*M*orag smelled delicious. She was cool, petite, and dark, with dark eyes and an intensity in her gaze that made me feel unsteady. Kind of like water that you knew was deep and dangerous despite the calm surface. But she was able to reach up to my lips, my ear, to whisper into it... it was as though she was all around me. Her hands on me, her body close to mine—it felt right. And while my entire world had fallen apart only last night, Morag felt more right than anything had in ages.

"I do," I whispered against her lips. I didn't want to pull away from her. I felt like I wanted to keep touching her, not move too far from her.

She did move away from me then, and my entire being cried out in protest. That was weird—at least, I thought it was. It had been so long since I'd had anything to do with girls. I'd had a few girls I flirted with, and kissed, among families of other Hunters. But my parents had taken me out of school in eighth grade, deeming the world of the "normal" something I didn't need exposure to. I'd been stubborn, making sure I graduated high school, completing a home school program, and then did the same thing with university. Online courses meant I had more time to be at home, training and practicing. Less time out in the world of the unaware, the normal, the forbidden.

Given all that I'd been taught, Morag would have been on the list of things forbidden. Not only did I not care, I welcomed it.

Morag took my hand and brought me along with her as she moved out the door. She was the most graceful woman I'd ever seen, and I'd grown up around women who fought for their lives regularly. She looked over her shoulder as we left the club. "You sure?"

I nodded. I'd never been more sure of anything in my entire life. She walked quickly, with great surety. This was a woman who knew her own mind and knew her place in the world. I envied that.

Mentally, I gave myself a kick. This was not the time to be moping and whining over what had happened. Although I did feel it was right to mourn. There would be a time to take a break for myself, so that I could clear my head and figure out what came next.

Tonight, however, was about this woman dragging

me along. For such a petite woman, her strength was incredible. I couldn't wait to get back to her place and— I stopped. "You're at a hotel?"

"I'm not from here," Morag said, her voice quiet and still with the background of the surrounding night.

Even more perfect. Two strangers, helping each other to—I didn't know what Morag was looking for. I'd thought I'd known what my direction was, my purpose. Now I had nothing. But maybe tonight, I could lose myself in this incredible woman, and forget everything.

Morag led the way into the hotel and into the lift. We were the only people moving in the lobby. Even the hotel desk was momentarily empty. Once the lift doors closed, she turned to me and pulled my head down to hers. Her mouth crashed into mine, her kiss full of power and need and hunger.

I liked it.

We kissed until the ding of the elevator reminded us that we needed to get off. I held back a snicker. We'd be getting off all right, if I had any say in the matter, but it was probably better if we weren't in the lift, or the middle of a hallway.

She led me down the bland hall to a room which she opened with the wave of her key. She was smooth— I hadn't seen her take the key out.

Once inside, she pushed me against the door, and kissed me, her tongue darting in and out of my mouth like someone who hadn't been kissed in years.

Oh, wait. That was me. But Morag kissed like I felt. Hungry. Demanding.

She pulled my jacket down, and I shrugged at it to conceal the knives within. I wasn't fast enough, and when Morag got it off me, the knives clanged. She looked in the inner pocket of the coat as she caught sight of my knives.

Grabbing my hand, she looked down at them. "Why do you have these?" She asked. There was a light edge to her voice. It made me feel good, as if she cared. If she didn't, she would have tossed aside my hands, and then told me to go fuck off. Right before she tossed me out of the room.

That's what I would have done, what most people would have done, and I felt like Morag and I were on the same level about a lot of things. I don't know why I felt that, but I did.

"These are nice," she said, looking at the blades without touching them. "Not really necessary at the moment, though," she smiled.

I grinned back. "No, not really." I kissed her, tugging at her shirt. She appreciated knives. Another point in her favor.

She pulled the tee shirt over my head and then undid the button on my jeans. She was so fast, I felt like I could barely catch my breath. My pants dropped to the floor.

When Morag saw that I didn't wear underwear, she smiled a smile that made my blood boil, and my cock stand at attention. Her gaze was approving. "Efficient," she said.

Her eyes moved over me. There was no hiding the large bruise on the side of my ribs. I'd iced it, but it was dark, standing out in high relief against my skin.

"Very," I replied. Her tee shirt came off, and then her jeans. She was the most beautiful woman I'd ever seen. The moon shone in through the window, and Morag was like cool marble, gleaming in the dark of the night. Her body was perfect.

She took my hand and led me to the bed. I caught a glimpse of her face. Her eyes were focused on me, but there was a small turn to her lips that was almost a smile. Something soft, which didn't quite fit with the rest of her.

She reached up to touch my face, her hand brushing against my cheek as I bent down to kiss her, one of my hands running down her smooth, cool body. Her other hand came up to curl into my hair, her nails scratching me lightly.

It made a shiver run through me. I wanted more, much, much more of this woman.

Morag gracefully lowered herself onto the bed, bringing me with her, still kissing me. I covered her with my body, loving how well our bodies fit together. When I nestled between her legs, it felt like... something familiar, something I'd known before, even as I knew I'd never met her.

Not much time when you're always training to be a

killer. The thought of all that I'd done, all that I'd been, sickened me, and I pushed it away. Plenty of time for that later. Right now, it was time to bury myself in the woman with me.

She was perfect.

Even better, she opened her legs wider to accommodate me, and I felt myself slide against her. "Hey," I said. "We need to—"

Morag reached over to the bedside table and handed me a small foil packet. "Right here."

I took it as I pushed back on my knees. Tearing it open, I rolled it on, and looked at her. "You sure?"

"Yes," she breathed, her eyes large and luminous, drawing me in.

"But—"

Morag reached up to touch my lips. "Chase," she said, her voice wrapping around my name and making me want her even more, "We have all night. I want you now."

Her words set me aflame. She was right. We did have all night. It thrilled me even more to know that she wanted me here, with her, all night.

"Yes, we do," I said, my voice husky. I kissed her, and she bit my bottom lip. Without hesitation, I thrust into her, taking her.

Morag's head fell back, her mouth open in an 'O' of pleasure.

*J*ust before dawn, Morag kissed me. I felt like I'd gone on the toughest raid of my life. I could feel the burn across my shoulders from her nails, and my body was tired, and finally, finally ready to sleep.

She slid from the bed as I reached for her. "Where are you going?" I asked.

"Just to clean up. Go to sleep." She smiled at me.

I was so tired. I let my eyes close as I heard her go into the bathroom.

CHAPTER FIVE

Morag

*W*hen I was sure Chase was asleep, I raced down to the front desk. The clerk looked startled at my appearance. "I need the room next to mine," I said. Glancing out the windows, I saw that I didn't have a lot of time. Dawn was coming.

"Um, what's your room number?" The clerk, who was a young man with spots still dotting his face, glanced nervously at me.

I gave him the number and took the key when he finally managed to add the room next door. I hadn't planned on meeting my mate. But I had. I wanted him to stay. Now, however, I needed to sleep. So another room, because I didn't need him finding me at rest in the closet.

That would put our chances of a successful match

somewhere between zero and hell to the no. Well, maybe not. I had a coven full of people who had done the same thing, and they'd managed to stay together. So there was hope.

Chase was amazing. I smiled as I raced into the room to see him sleeping, his breath a whisper in the darkened room. I leaned down to kiss him. He mumbled something, reaching for me.

Reluctantly moving away, I found the notepad that was on the desk. I couldn't afford to let him draw me in now. If I crawled back into bed with him, I'd never want to leave. I wrote a note, and placed it on his jacket.

Which made me think of the knives. Why did he carry such lethal knives? There was more to my mate than met the eye. The air of danger I'd sensed on him hadn't been mere wishful thinking on my part. There was something he was involved in that made him feel the need to carry them.

The knives might have something to do with the bruise the size of Britain on his side, and the smaller bruises along his lower back. He looked like someone had recently kicked the shit out of him.

There were also lash marks on his back. As in, someone had whipped him. Yes, there was something dangerous and dark about my mate. The thought thrilled me even as I was angered that someone had hurt him. Which said something about me, as well, but I didn't care.

I'd discover that later. With a last look at him, I

25

turned and went through the connecting door, locking it on my side. Hurrying, I pulled blankets and cushions from the couch into the closet, and shut the door behind me just as daylight was peeking through the curtains.

As I closed my eyes, I relived the night I'd spent with my mate. I was no stranger to men. I loved them, in fact. But this—being with my mate—was like nothing I'd ever experienced before. My heart beat slowed, falling in time with his. With Chase.

Sleep came over me. I didn't fall into the deeper sleep I was accustomed to, and for a moment, I felt a flash of panic. What was wrong? I listened, waiting.

And heard my heart beat. It was my Chase. My mate's heart would not let me abandon him, even as I had to take my rest.

The thought made me so happy, I almost didn't recognize it. This. This was happiness. Finding the one person meant for you—and I'd found it.

Now how to tell him? That was the tricky, hundred-thousand dollar question. I'd watched my coven mates tell their mates, and the reactions were much like you'd expect. One was calm, another decidedly not, and the rest were in between.

That is, if Chase was still here when I rose later tonight. I'd asked him to stay in my note, telling him I had to work, but would be back later today—I had no idea whether he would stay or go. When I'd first seen him, I had no intention of anything other than spending the night with him and then booting him out and getting some rest.

The beat of my heart made that all different. He had to stay.

There had never been a case that I knew of where a vampire met their mate and their mate walked away. In some cases, it took some time for the mate to accept what was happening. I found the idea that the fates had chosen one person for you exciting. Not everyone saw it that way at first. But leaving?

I'd never seen it. I hoped I wouldn't be that one vampire who was different. The thought made me feel panicked and worried and want to get up to go make sure Chase was still there.

But I couldn't.

I could only feel my heart beating and know that he was close by.

How to tell him? I had no fucking idea. None. Now I wished I'd paid attention when my coven mates had been moaning on about how they met—having no mate, and no prospects, I'd tuned out.

Looked like karma was having a bit of a laugh at my expense. That's what I got for not paying attention.

While I didn't need to breathe, I forced myself to inhale and exhale, to focus on the breath, and my beating heart, and stop my worries. There was nothing I could do until it was night again. What would happen today was going to happen regardless of how much I worried over it.

I knew, though, that if he was gone, I'd have to go find him. There was nothing else I could do. There was no way I could let him walk away.

My sleep was restless. I opened my eyes before it was full night, waiting. Listening to my heart beat—but it was fainter now. Why? Was Chase gone?

Damn it all. Pacing in my closet, I wondered where he could have gone. Why he'd gone—what if he didn't feel our connection?

Jesus. Not only would I need to explain the vampire thing, and the mating thing, but the idea that he was it for me. That I was it for him. How?

If I could still sweat, I'd be sweating hard right now. When it was dusk, I shot out of the closet into the bathroom. I could get ready, even if I couldn't leave yet. After the fastest shower I'd ever taken and getting myself together—I noted that I took extra care with my hair—I waited for the dark to fall.

The second it was safe, I was out of my room and unlocking the door in the room where I'd left him. I couldn't hear anything, so I crossed my fingers that he would still be there. I burst through the door, looking around.

Chase was sitting on the small sofa, a burger halfway to his mouth. He lowered the burger. "Morag. You came back."

"I said I would."

He smiled a little ruefully. "People say lots of things as they're leaving."

I felt myself relax a little. He was here. He hadn't left. He wanted to see me again.

"I had to work. Why wouldn't I come back?" I walked to the other side of the sofa and sat next to him. "You were incredible."

Chase blushed. "So were you."

There was not a moment in my long life where I'd ever felt happier than hearing those words from my mate's mouth.

"Go ahead and eat. I'm sorry I interrupted," I said, gesturing at the burger.

"You want some? Shit, I didn't get any for you—" he stopped, looking horrified.

"No, I ate while I was out." I'd need to eat tomorrow. After I was able to get a better sense of how things were going to go with Chase.

"You're sure?"

He was so... so... adorable in his concern. Even thinking the thought made me both delighted and ready to throw up in my own mouth. Everything I'd ever teased my coven mates about was happening, just as they said it was.

I would never live this down.

But if I had Chase with me, it didn't matter. He was worth it.

Chase took a bite of his burger and chewed. I'd forgotten how loud other people eating could be. When he swallowed, he said, "I slept the entire day. I'm not as —" he stopped, a look I couldn't decipher crossing his face. "I guess I was tired," he finished.

That had not been what he wanted to say. He was hiding something.

"Sometimes it's necessary," I said. We had time to share secrets. Besides, I really wasn't one to cast stones. He hadn't seen my fangs yet.

"Yeah, I guess so," Chase took another bite of the burger.

"So you're not from Edinburgh either?" I asked, looking around for a safe topic.

"No, we live out in the country. South of here. We're..." he stopped again. "My parents are pretty private," he finished.

"There's nothing wrong with that," I said. "My family lives on the Isle of Mull, in an old castle, with no neighbors close by."

"At least you have neighbors," Chase said. His words were almost bitter.

Interesting. Something to file away to ask about later. As for now, I shrugged. "What do you do?" I asked. Could this conversation get any more inane?

"Uh... well, I work in the family business."

"A business that requires you to carry around deadly weapons?" I asked. Not that I minded. I actually approved. "Don't let the coppers catch you with those," I grinned.

"Yes, well," he took another bite of his burger. He ate quickly. When he'd finished, he said, "I'm sorry I didn't wait for you for dinner."

"That's no worry," I said. I was good for the next few days. His concern was touching. "I rather thought we'd spend time here," I said, smiling slightly.

"That sounds perfect," Chase said, getting up to toss the remains of his dinner. "What did you have in mind? A movie?"

I just looked at him. Was he kidding?

"I'm joking," he said, laughing. "Your expression is priceless."

I smiled. This would take some getting used to. "Then what did you have in mind?" I asked.

"Something like this," Chase came up to me, and wrapped his arms around me from behind. He leaned down to kiss my neck as his hands grabbed my hips and he pressed himself against me. He felt so good.

"Really? This might be... suitable," I said, tilting my head to allow him better access to my neck.

He kissed from my jaw down to my shoulder, his lips soft and leaving a trail of desire as he kissed me. My heart sped up as his did. God, did I want him to bite me. Right where the shoulder met the neck. I wanted to feel his heart race as he bit down—feeling what he felt was just as everything else.

He stepped back and pulled off my shirt. "You are so beautiful," he said, pushing my hair aside to kiss the back of my neck.

A shiver ran through my entire body.

"I'm so glad you came back."

"I wanted to," I said, my voice breathless.

31

His hands cupped my breasts, sliding the bra up, and pinching at my nipples. I arched into him, loving the feel of his hands on me. I wanted him right now, right this instant. I made to turn around but his hands held me in place in front of him. He removed my bra and tweaked my nipples again. It felt fantastic even as the teasing touch was making me crazy.

I stopped moving, and Chase's hands moved to my pants. Unbuttoning them, he slid them down, going to his knees behind me.

He kissed the small of my back. Then slowly, kissing me along my waist, he turned me around, and kissed my belly. Now I faced him, in only ridiculously lacy panties. Panties I'd chosen with him in mind.

Chase looked up at me, and the look in his eyes was the most sensual thing I'd ever seen in my entire life, human or vampire. I reached down to cup his face, my hands on his cheeks. He turned his face and kissed one of my hands.

He pulled down my panties. I put a hand on his shoulder as I stepped out of them. Chase tossed them aside. He kissed me, letting his tongue run between my legs. I felt my entire body tense at his touch. Chase pushed my legs open, giving him greater access to me. He licked and sucked at me as my hands anchored themselves in his hair.

He sucked harder, and I felt my fangs drop. I closed my mouth tightly over them and felt the warm taste of blood as I bit my lip.

When Chase slipped one, then two fingers inside me, never stopping what he was doing with his mouth, my head fell back and I moaned. I could feel myself getting close; I'd have to make sure I didn't bite him as I came. I wanted to taste him so badly.

Our hearts were beating wildly, and then Chase bit me, and I lost all control, crying out and pulling at his hair. My orgasm washed over me with the strength of a tidal wave. I didn't feel steady, which was born out a moment later as I fell onto him and we both ended up on the floor.

CHAPTER SIX

Chase

*H*earing Morag come because I was between her legs and making her come—it was so sexy I nearly came myself. When she fell forward onto me, I wrapped my arms around her, grabbing onto her ass, and ground my cock into her. She kissed me hungrily. Then, with one graceful move, she pushed herself off me and unbuttoned my jeans. Pulling them down, she smiled when she saw that once more, I had no underwear, and just like last night, I was hard as a rock.

Morag carefully pulled the jeans off me and got up. As she came back, she was tearing open a small foil packet. She crouched over me, and rolled it on, and before I could even say anything, positioned herself over me, and lowered her body onto my cock.

This felt like coming home.

What?

Get it together, Robson, I thought. You're up to the eyeballs with the most beautiful woman in the world. Focus.

Morag moved up and down, slowly. I noticed that she was balancing on her feet, not touching my sides.

She'd seen the bruises. So she made sure not to touch them. Watching her move showed me she was deliberately working not to hurt me further.

A rush of—I wasn't sure what—rolled over me in waves, and I couldn't get enough of her. I placed my hands on her hips, thrusting up as I did, bruises be damned. She bore down on me, and we moved together, slowly and then faster and faster. Her skin felt smooth under my hands, and her hair fell into her face. But she never took her eyes from me.

And then, before I really knew it, I was coming, holding her to me with all my strength. I said something, although I didn't know what the hell it was and wouldn't be able to repeat it if my life depended on it. Morag was quiet, never taking her eyes from me.

It felt more intimate than anything I'd ever done with another person. I stared, not sure what to say. "Wow," I managed.

She smiled, leaning down to kiss me. "Wow, yourself." Carefully, she stood up.

I got up with a lot less grace and headed for the bathroom.

When I came out, Morag was in bed, the sheet up around her chest. "Come lie with me," she said, patting the bed next to her.

"I could go for another burger."

"Then let's order you one," she said, reaching for the phone.

"You're not hungry?" I asked. She'd only ordered one.

"No, I had to eat at work. With clients," she smiled. "But don't let me stop you."

"I won't. I need to keep up my strength," I grinned at her.

"Oh, good. I was worried you'd pass out early," she laughed.

"What's early?"

"Anything before dawn," Morag grinned wickedly at me.

My cock twitched. "You mean all night?" I asked.

"I hope so." Her eyebrow went up.

"You sure you don't want anything to eat? You're not getting any sleep until the sun comes up," I said, reaching under the sheet and running my hand down her body and between her legs.

"I think I'm up for the challenge," she said, her hand doing some wandering of its own.

We lay together, stroking and teasing one another. I loved the way she felt next to me, tucked into my arm.

The knock on the door surprised us, and she

grabbed the sheet from the bed with a vicious yank, wrapping it around her. The server brought the tray in, and set it down on the desk, keeping his eyes lowered, looking all sorts of uncomfortable as he did so.

Once Morag signed for it, and he left, we both burst into laughter.

I'd never eaten so fast in recent memory as I did then.

And we spent the entire night exploring one another. The sight of Morag with her head back, her long neck exposed, glowing in the moonlight, was seared into my memory.

Just as the sky was lightening outside the window, she kissed me. "Get some sleep. I may need to go out to work today, so if I'm not here, I'll be back later."

"Okay," I said, curling into her back, wrapping my arms around her waist and snugging her to me. She sighed, and I felt her relax.

Closing my eyes, I thought about how I'd never been so happy, and how I'd need to tell her the truth about me, because I wanted to see her again after this weekend.

Sleep was drifting over me as I wondered how the hell you explained vampires, and my job, to normal people.

~

I opened my eyes to shadows on the wall from the darkening sky. Sitting up, I looked at the clock. I'd slept all day. "Morag?" I said.

The room was quiet. She must have gone out. That was a good thing. I needed time to shower and clean up. I also needed a long, hot shower.

I came out of the bathroom with a towel wrapped around me.

"That's a good look on you," I heard.

I whirled around, going into a fighting crouch.

Morag was sitting on the bed, looking at me like I'd grown another head.

"Uh, sorry," I said. "You startled me."

"What do you do?" she asked. Her face and voice were expressionless.

"I told you, remember? Family business." I made a show of rolling my eyes. I could feel my heart beat faster, hoping she wouldn't ask more.

"Can I see your knives?" Morag got up abruptly, going to where my jacket lay across the desk.

"Sure," I said. "They're sharp, though."

"I'll be careful," she said, her voice sounding odd as she turned her back to me.

She reached into my pocket and pulled out a knife. Then she hissed, sounding like the angriest cat ever, and dropped the knife to the floor. Morag clutched at her hand as she turned to look at me. "Why do you have silver knives, Chase?"

38

"For hunting," I replied automatically. I could feel the sweat bead down my back. Why was she so upset about the knives? Something tickled the back of my brain but—

"What do you hunt?" Morag asked, sounding hard and angry.

"I just use them for work," I managed finally.

Why hadn't my parents trained me for this? For how to discuss what I did? This very instant, this moment right here, this was why they kept us away from the rest of the world.

There was no good way to share this, share what my family did.

Probably why Hunters married other Hunters. For one thing, it was easier.

Another thought hit me. "How did you know they were silver?" I asked. While my knives were gorgeous, I didn't advertise the fact they were silver. Some punk would have tried to bean me over the head and steal them. I tried not to inflict damage on normal people, or draw attention to myself.

"What are you?" Morag whispered. Her voice was ragged, almost broken sounding. Why should my knives do that to her?

"I'm a hunter," I said. "You know, game hunting? That's the family business."

"And you need silver knives?"

I nearly missed the question, since she was whispering, but her words carried in the quiet of the room.

When I didn't answer, Morag spoke again. "They are shit for hunting, Chase. Silver is malleable." She rubbed at her hand.

Oh, shit. This conversation, with no help from me, had completely gone off the rails. "It's complicated," I said, stalling.

"What do you hunt, Chase?"

I opened my mouth and closed it. Why was her hand burned?

"What do you hunt?" Her voice was hard.

"Things you don't have to worry about," I said. A thought hit me and I nearly fell over. No. That was crazy. I shoved it aside.

"You sure about that?" Morag backed away from my coat, sitting down in the chair near the desk. "What do you hunt?"

"Things that don't like silver," I said.

Morag stared at me. Her mouth dropped open a little, and oddly, she put her hand to where her heart was. Her eyes closed.

Okay, what I did wasn't great, but she didn't know that. Her reactions seemed wrong, overdone.

"It's not that big of a deal," I said, sitting down on the bed. "Come back and sit with me."

"I'll be right back," she said, getting up from the chair and going to the connecting door. Before I could say anything, she disappeared through the door. Since when did she have another room?

"What the hell just happened?" I asked the empty room. Something was wrong, I just needed to figure out what.

My phone rang. Oh, shit. I'd turned it back on when I went out to get a burger earlier, and forgotten to turn it off.

"No," I whispered, and then I turned it over to see who it was, even though I already knew. I was hoping I was wrong. But I'd seen all the missed calls.

As expected, it was my dad.

"Hello?" I answered it, knowing if I didn't, he'd keep calling.

"Where are you?"

"I'm taking a break," I said firmly.

"There are no breaks in this business," Dad shot back. "Get home. We have work to do. There's been trouble. You're needed. You need to fix your mess."

"No, I'm going to be gone for a few days," I said. "You're damn right there's trouble. Trouble you brought."

"Grow up and be a man," Dad growled at me. "You don't get time off because you want it." I could hear the sneer in his tone. "There's things that need doing, and you don't get to—"

I cut him off. "Well, I'm a grown man, and I'm taking time off. I'll call you when I'm on my way back." I ended the call.

It was a good thing I'd turned off my GPS on my

phone last night. While he hadn't said anything, I was pretty sure that the lack of a GPS signal was the only reason he wasn't banging on my door and dragging me out of here.

And I couldn't leave now. Not when I'd met Morag. There was something here, something more than just sex, although the sex was the most amazing sex I'd ever had.

There wasn't a lot to compare her to, but I knew, instinctively, that this woman was amazing. And special. Whether it was just her, or the two of us together, I wasn't sure. Although I felt strongly that a lot of this was Morag. She exuded strength, and confidence. I'd grown up around strong, capable, fierce women. She was all of those things.

When I'd come to Edinburgh to take time for myself, to manage the truth I now knew, I had no idea I'd meet someone who felt so right. But I had. And I had to see where this went.

The door between rooms opened. "Why'd you get another room?" I got up, wanting to feel her close to me, but she put out a hand.

"Because I needed another room, Chase. You need to tell me now. What is your family business?" This Morag in front of me had no trace of the woman I'd spent the last night in bed with. She was deadly serious.

"What does it matter?" I threw up my hands. I didn't want to talk about the damn family business. Not now, and sure as hell not in a towel.

"What does it matter?" Morag's face shifted, and there was an incredible sadness on her. "It matters because of this." She opened her mouth and her fangs dropped down.

CHAPTER SEVEN

Morag

We stared at one another, me with my fangs out, his heart beating, and my heart thumping in concert. If I could have cried human tears, I would have. My mate was a Hunter. A Hunter. He killed my kind. Had I been able to hold his silver knives, I would have smelled the blood of now-dead vampires on it. I knew it, as sure as I knew anything.

"You're a Hunter," I breathed. The best looking man I'd ever seen, still wet from the shower, wrapped in only a towel, standing in front of me, and... the kind of man who killed those like me.

His eyes widened. "How did you know? And you're a vampire? Of course," he nodded as though something had been confirmed for him.

"Yeah. Fangs? Sleep all day? You know, why I've

been gone the last two days?" I rolled my eyes. It was only two days, and my entire world had shifted.

"I thought you were working," he said. Then he shook his head. "Of course," he said again. "Why did you come up to me at the bar, then?"

"Because... "I stopped and looked away. How could this be my mate? How? A Hunter? "Because something in you called to me." That was as close as I could come to the truth right now.

"It's not just me, then," Chase said, sitting back down on the bed. "There's something here, something between us."

"You feel it?" I was amazed.

He nodded.

"When were you going to tell me you are a Hunter?" I asked.

"I don't know..." he looked away. "I'm not proud of it."

"Then why do you do it?" I whispered.

"I wasn't kidding about the family business. It's all I've ever known."

The waves of pain rushed through me. We all knew that Hunters were still here. I heard about vampires disappearing.

"Why are you here? Are you working now?" I asked, my voice a whisper. My heart beat faster, because Chase's was beating faster. I didn't want to have to —

He looked down. "Yes. Well, no. Not for you!" He held up a hand at my shocked look. "I'm supposed to be working, but I said sod it, and came here instead. The raid was..." he stopped, thinking. "The raid was Wednesday, two days ago. It's been a while since we'd done a raid. Vampires are smart."

"Of course we are," I snapped. "You think we don't know about you?"

"I... uh... I don't know what I think anymore," Chase said. He looked ashamed.

As he should be.

"And how many did you take down this week?" I snarled, my anger rising up and protecting my pain.

"There were children," he whispered.

"What?" I asked. My anger was forgotten, replaced by shock. Children were so rare. Vampires wouldn't turn a child. But they could be born.

"I'd never... Jesus, do you want to hear this?" He looked up, and I saw in his face why he'd come to the bar. Why he'd had desperation all around him.

"I do," I sat down in the chair at the desk, a safe distance from him. His jacket with the knives was closer to me than him, and if he went for it—I'd take him down. I couldn't believe it. I couldn't believe he'd fooled me, that I hadn't been able to tell.

"We are always training," Chase said, looking off at the wall. "Ever since I was little, it was always training. The only reason I got any kind of education is because I forced my parents to let me. Everything online, of course. Can't take away from the training," his voice deepened, and I wondered if it was his father's voice he heard when he spoke. "I wasn't a hardcore believer anymore, but... I didn't have the strength to leave. And... well, it doesn't matter." He looked down at his hands, clasped in front of him.

He met my eyes. "So we planned this week carefully. The coven was about fifteen members, from what we could tell. They kept to themselves. You can usually find vampires because of suspicious deaths in the area, but this coven hid itself well."

I made a noise but didn't say anything. His words were why Collum was so careful. In this day and age, it made sense to find a blood bank, and order blood. Or a willing donor. Those were available as well. Or take a sip here and there, in a crowd. Never too much. Not as exciting, but safer. Sensible.

"We came upon the coven during the day, but there must have been some who were able to be awake, to hide, because it took longer than my dad and the other leaders thought it should to find all the vampires. There were two other Hunter families. A big group. They pulled all the vampires out of their sleeping places, and they..." he stopped. "My father, and my two brothers, some of the others," he dropped his head.

"Yes?" My voice was hard.

"They tortured them," he whispered. "In a fight, to kill your enemy is not a bad thing, and you do it quickly. Cleanly. There's no need to make anyone suffer. But they... they hurt them, laughing, enjoying themselves, making sure they all suffered, and then killed them. It turned my stomach. The screams..."

"What happened to the children?" I ground out.

"Some of the women got away. The kids were with them. That was my job, to find the women. I didn't expect to see children, because the intel seemed unreliable, and I was so surprised. One of the women knocked me down and she and another woman ran past me carrying two kids." His eyes met mine, and I could see that he was haunted by his memories. "My father screamed not to let the bitches and whelps go, but I couldn't get up fast enough."

"Did he do that to you?" I pointed at his torso. The marks on his back were obvious, and I'd noted them when we'd been together, but hadn't said anything.

Chase nodded. "Yes. The rest of the Hunters we were with had tied up the vampires they'd found with silver-plated wire. They were torturing them, and my dad and brothers were part of it. One of the woman..." He stopped. "She screamed as they dragged out one of the vampires, a name, I think."

"What was the name?" I asked. I knew of the covens near us.

"I couldn't hear, but my father and one of the other men had a vampire they were pulling along, and she had long, silvery hair." He looked down.

I felt his heart as he relived the moment, and my own breath caught. I knew of a vampire with that hair. I didn't know there were children in her coven, though. It made sense to keep them hidden, and I wondered how the Hunters had discovered them.

"When they realized the women and kids had gotten away, that I hadn't caught them, Jeffrey, one of the other leaders, told my dad they needed to be found. Dad ordered my brothers and I to come with him, so we could go and clean up the mess that I'd made. He said that my mistake was on all of us. My dad gave me ten lashes, to drive the point home." He sounded bitter.

"We all went in different directions, but not before my father had my brothers beat the hell out of me, so this time I wouldn't forget what I was supposed to be about. Dad mostly stood by, watching, looking satisfied. But after he told me where I was supposed to be searching, I made a decision. I left. I couldn't stay there. All my life, my mother told me that we were doing good work, keeping people safe. That might have been true at some point, although I'm having my doubts. But this? This was my father taking out anger and hate on another being. This was hurting for the fun of it."

"You don't think that kind of goes along with being a Hunter?" I asked, unable to keep the sarcasm from my voice.

"Have you killed humans for food?" Chase asked, and there was a hardness in his question. He looked me right in the eye, not giving an inch, looking every bit as fierce and dangerous as I'd sensed he was when I met him.

Damn it. Why'd he have to look so good? Why did my body and heart not care what he was?

Chase continued, "If you have, you have no room to give me hell. We both have killed for what we thought were good reasons."

"I killed to eat. You killed because you hate," I shot back. As angry as I was, I was glad to see him fighting back. Even if he was so far beyond wrong.

"Or because I didn't want to be eaten. I didn't want others to be eaten." He was getting mad now.

"How many vampires ever came after you?" I stood up.

"How many humans bothered you?" Chase's voice rose.

"Plenty!" I yelled. "Anything different, anything out of the norm—and it was blame those strange folk on the hill! Let's go to their house and burn it down! We have to spend our whole lives in hiding!"

"Because you're killers!" Chase stood up, yelling right back at me.

"So are you," I said quietly. "And you don't even eat what you kill."

We stared at one another, the anger breaking all that had gone before between us.

CHAPTER EIGHT

Chase

I could not believe that Morag was a vampire. How had I missed it? She had cool skin. But she wasn't cold. If anything, she'd been warm and—my cheeks felt hot as I thought of the last two nights. She was fast, faster than normal people.

And the fangs! How had I missed the fangs? What would my family say? What would my dad say? He'd beat me senseless if I went home and told him I'd slept with a vampire.

It hit me that I was dealing with an awful lot of violence at the hands of my family. That was something to deal with—later. Now, I needed to focus on Morag.

But... but Morag didn't feel evil. She didn't feel like some kind of demon come to Earth, which is what I'd always been taught. She was sexy and moved with a grace I'd never noticed in vampires before. She was kind. I knew she'd seen my bruises, and the lash marks on my back. She hadn't said a word. She'd actually managed to avoid touching any of them.

"This is a disaster. A fucking unmitigated disaster," she walked away from me to pace on the other side of the room, close to the connecting door. Her hand went up to run through her hair, and I wondered if she was aware of it.

"No, it's not. We just go our separate ways. No one else ever has to know," I said, even as the thought of never seeing her again made something in me rage and want to break down and cry at the same time. I didn't want to go our separate ways, but what else could we do?

"You don't understand," Morag said. She looked at me, and I could see that some sort of war was going on within her. Over what, I couldn't tell.

"Then explain it to me," I said.

"You're the one," she snarled.

"The one what? What does that mean?"

"I can feel you, in here!" She hit herself on the chest. "When I got close to you, I could feel your heartbeat. It makes my heart beat."

"Can't you feel everyone's heartbeat?" I wasn't understanding.

"No. The only time a vampire's heart beats is when they meet their mate."

"What?" I heard what she said, but I couldn't take it in.

"You. Are. My. Mate."

"Um... what?" I seemed stuck as to a choice for words. "What if I don't want to be?"

Morag glared.

"We're not exactly all simpatico," I said, rolling my eyes. Actually, we were, if you left out the Hunter and vampire aspects. Why was I fighting this when all I wanted was to be with her?

"That doesn't matter."

"What does it mean, this mate thing?"

"It means we are tied together forever," she said. "Unless one of us dies."

She glanced at my jacket, which held my knives, and the room stilled around us. I held out a hand as I looked at the jacket and then back at her.

Morag gasped, and she rushed me. I put up my hands, but her fist shot out and hit me in the face. My nose exploded in pain as I saw stars.

"Ow! Damn it all, woman!" I roared, reaching for her, but she wasn't there. I felt the towel drop away from my waist as I felt the blood rush down my face.

"Great," I snarled.

I staggered to the bathroom to get another towel and held it to my nose. Blinking to help the stars in my eyes clear, I leaned my hand against the sink with my other hand.

"Morag!" I shouted.

There was no response. I made it to the connecting door which was open. "Morag!"

She wasn't in the other room, either.

She was gone.

"How in the hell?" I asked the empty rooms, but I knew. I'd seen vampires move. They were so fast that human eyes couldn't keep up with them.

"Morag!" I yelled. I knew that vampires had keen hearing—if she was still close enough, she might hear me. "Don't leave!"

I waited, the silence of the room mocking me. "Morag, please," I said.

There was no answer.

She was gone.

I sat on the bed, my head whirling. There was a lot to process, and I needed to organize, and plan. There was no way I was letting Morag go. Before she told me about the mate thing, I wanted to spend more time with her. Now that I knew we were meant to be together, I wasn't letting her just walk away.

How the hell was that supposed to happen, though? A Hunter, and a vampire?

My family would disown me. Who knew what hers would do? I assumed she had a coven, since she'd mentioned her family.

Her family. Wait—where had she said she was from? I rubbed my temples, trying to remember.

She'd said... the Isle of Mull! That was it. The Isle of Mull. What else had she said? A castle, an old castle.

I pulled out my phone and checked on the distance. I'd have to get to Oban, get a ferry.

Then I stopped. I was taking my life into my hands. She had a coven. If she told them about me—they might kill me before I ever got to see her.

Was she worth it?

I thought back to the past two nights we'd spent together. Morag had been all in, willing to laugh, and be rough, and playful, and gentle—she'd avoided all my bruises, even though she'd not said a word—and I'd come so hard I thought my head was going to explode. I *liked* her. I felt comfortable with her in a way I didn't feel comfortable around anyone. Certainly not my family, what with the beatings being a regular form of communication in times of strife.

Was she the one for me? I didn't know. But the way she talked about this bond, being mates—it was apparent that this was a normal occurrence in vampire land. So there must be something that made fate, or kismet, or whatever—choose to make her heart beat because of me. I'd like the chance to find out.

Yeah, that was worth it.

A saying my mother had told me when I was getting interested in girls popped back into my head. "It's when people are naked before you that you see them the most. You see them at their best, and at their worst."

I hadn't seen the worst of Morag. It was there. I was sure of it. But she hadn't killed me, or attacked me, barring the punch to the face which I understood, even as my nose still hurt. She'd done it to get away.

Knowing that she could have killed me made it poignant.

Which made me laugh out loud, despite how fast this had fallen right into cluster fuck territory. Only a Hunter could see a vampire breaking their nose as poignant.

As I went back to find my pants, I staggered, dropping to my knees. My heart felt as though it had been ripped out, and I had to work to catch my breath, with a bleeding nose and a towel on my face.

"What is this?" I asked out loud. My chest ached so badly. I rubbed at it, trying to at least dull the ache.

It didn't help. First things firsts. Pants for sure. Then stop the damn bleeding. Then find Morag. My Morag. Well, she could be my Morag.

My mate. At that thought, my chest ached.

I got myself together despite the pain and headed out. I needed to get my motorcycle and get on the road. The ferries waited for no one, and I had a ferry to catch.

CHAPTER NINE

Morag

I could feel the tears at the edge of my eyes, and I brushed at my face angrily, not bothering to be gentle. Then I rubbed at my chest where my traitorous heart still beat, and where an ache was spreading like a virus from my center. Rubbing didn't do shit. I hurt. It hurt to leave Chase as I had. It hurt to punch him in his nose. Even though I wasn't sure whether he was going for his knives or not—I had to get away. And punching him in the nose seemed the best bet on short notice.

But still, it hurt. Like, physically hurt.

Drops of blood from where I'd hit him lingered on the leather of my jacket. I resisted the urge to lick them, to taste him. But I couldn't. I'd lose all my strength and go running back to him.

Which reminded me I needed to eat. But I didn't have the heart for it. My heart was already full of someone else.

Damn Chase Robson. Damn fate, too, while I was at it. Why in the name of all the gods did fate see fit to match me with a Hunter? And not only that, a Hunter who'd just come back from a raid. A raid that I was pretty sure was on a coven I knew.

I ran in the night. I'd have to make it to the coast before dawn and see if a boat was headed toward Mull. I needed to get back, to see who had died, and to find a way to start putting the memory of Chase away.

Which could prove to be difficult. My heart was still beating, although it was fainter, softer. I wondered if that was because I was moving away from him. It also beat with an ache, like the finish from a taste of wine.

Sweet Jesus. Would my heart beat for as long as he was alive? The thought was so disturbing I stumbled as I ran, falling to my hands and knees.

"Wonderful," I grumbled. I got up, brushing myself off. Now I was falling and losing balance because of him. Why? Why did a Hunter have to be my mate? The question was a non-stop loop in my head, mixed with images of Chase naked.

Not a good combo. Not a good fucking combo at all.

I stretched for a moment before continuing, the faint beating of my heart nothing more than a knife that hit me over and over. While the beat was fainter, it hurt with each thump. Was that because we'd parted?

Holy hell. It needed to stop. I needed to see how to break a mating tie. I didn't even know if it was possible while both still lived.

That could possibly mean that one of us had to die. I couldn't kill Chase, so... I shook my head. I wasn't ready to die, but... I didn't know how long I could stand hearing my heart beat for the next fifty years. Or feeling the pain of not being with him.

And if he took a wife?

Rage washed over me, coloring everything red, making all my muscles tense. I shook my head and found that my body had gone into a defensive crouch.

"Wonderful," I said again. Thank goodness there was no one around to see me as I'd not only nearly fallen on my face in the middle of a field, I looked ready to rip someone's arm off and beat them with it. I started to run again, but with less speed, less energy. I was leaving my heart behind, even as it felt like it was broken. I'd left him. Every fiber of me screamed that I needed to go back, but I couldn't.

Because I didn't want to kill him, and when he spoke, I could see the faces of those he gave the final death to.

He didn't hurt the women and children, though. At least not on the last raid. So he said.

I wondered how truly effective the Hunters were. We always heard when raids happened. Most were not that successful. The Hunters unfortunately got one or two vampires—which was one or two too many—but most of the covens were able to escape. How had the Hunters been lucky enough to get more than a couple and torture them? That was a concern that would need some attention. Although not right now.

There hadn't been any word of covens with children. Vampires—usually mated vampires—could have children. But born vampires were rare. Although if there were children, it would make sense not to make it common knowledge, so they could reach maturity. Collum's sire, the vampire who had nearly killed him, until Isabeau saved him—he'd been born. From everything I'd read, and from what Collum shared, he'd been overly proud of the fact, too. Downright snotty, even.

Nevertheless, it didn't change what Chase did. What he *was*.

As I ran, I let the tears fall. I needed to grieve, and mourn, and get this out of my system. Because then I needed to either find a way to stop feeling his heart. If I couldn't, I wasn't sure I'd be able to go on.

I looked to the sky and realized that I'd been so slow that I was going to miss finding a boat before daylight. Damn it. I'd need to find a barn to bed down in, and that meant dirt. Some vampires enjoyed going to ground, literally, but I wasn't one of them.

Sighing, I began sizing up the buildings I was passing. If I remembered correctly, there was a ferry that did a run after night fell. I could have just dived in the water and swam to Mull, but I hated the sea between the mainland and the island. And the smell. I liked the smell from the beach, not on my person. Not to mention, I wasn't ready to face my coven.

This weekend had been a shitstorm, from beginning to end. All I'd wanted was to find someone to spend a night or two with and be able to go back to my coven without rolling my eyes at all the mated couples. Instead, my entire life, the rest of my life as a vampire, had been changed.

As I dug a hole for myself in a barn that seemed abandoned—I hoped, because I was not in the mood to be discovered—I tried to stop the images that played in my mind. Chase over top of me as we joined.

The feel of the sweat in the small of his back, making his skin slick and smooth.

How he ignored the bruises that hurt him as we moved together throughout the night.

The way he looked at me as we both found release. The way he gazed up at me when he knelt before me.

That was the worst. The look in his eyes. He hadn't known of the mating bond, but he'd felt it. It showed through his eyes.

Tears leaked from my eyes *again*, and I wiped my face carefully as I lay in my hole and began to cover myself with dirt. I didn't need gritty eyes when I woke tonight. I had enough to be dealing with.

Thankfully, I passed the day quietly. Like before, I didn't truly sleep. The beat of Chase's heart and my own answering heartbeat didn't allow me to. The barn was abandoned, because no one and no animal disturbed me. When I woke, I spent time brushing the dirt from me, and then ran down to the Oban ferry docks. I paid my fare, ignoring the looks I was getting. I knew I looked a bit shabby. There was nothing to be done about that.

The ferry ride seemed to take forever. I stood at the bow, watching the waves in the darkness as the island got closer. As the ferry docked, I was one of the first in line to disembark. I walked quickly away from the docks and once I'd left them, I began to run. It wouldn't take me long to get back to the house. Well, the castle, really.

The MacLean house was Lochdon House, and it had been in Collum's family for years. He'd heard of the direct line dying off some two hundred-plus years ago, and he'd bought it, bringing all of us together. It was a small castle, so the previous owners had called it Lochdon House, probably wanting to keep themselves from being seen as too uppity or prideful.

The castle was on a hill, set up high with no neighbors around us. The location allowed us to see all around. Fear of an attack was not so much of a concern now, but when it was built, and then when Collum took it over, being attacked was still a possibility.

I ran up the hill, and something made me stop. I kept completely still, listening. Without thinking, my hand went up to rub where my heart was. The ache hadn't subsided. But it had lessened. And what I heard —it couldn't be!

"Oh, for the love of all the saints," I groaned, and ran as fast as I could toward home.

CHAPTER TEN

Chase

*A*s I drove my motorcycle up the hill to Lochdon House, I hoped that my intelligence was correct. I'd done some reading about castles on the Isle of Mull, and while there were a few that seemed like they'd be considered castles, all but one were hotels, or bed-and-breakfast places.

Lochdon House was it as far as private residences went.

I snooped a little on social media, and found no one who lived there, although there was some discussion in the Mull Community Group about the MacLean family who still owned it.

It was my best bet, my best hope.

"Dear Lord, please don't let me get killed before I get a chance to try to sort this," I muttered. I took a few breaths. After Morag had punched me and left, I found that I ached all over. It was centered around my heart, but I felt like shit in general. More than I should, even with all that had happened.

Shutting off the motorcycle, I stood and stretched, taking it in. It was a castle. A small one, but a castle. There were lights on in some of the windows, but I had the impression that both the inhabitants and the house itself were waiting to see what I'd do.

As to that, I'd been thinking about it all the way here. I really, really didn't want to die, so I decided that I'd be out in the open, a ready target.

"Hello, the house!" It was an old-fashioned greeting but one we still used as Hunters when we went to visit other Hunter families. It allowed for the people within to get a look at you, decide whether you were a danger.

As there were probably older vampires here, they'd recognize it for what it was.

At least, I hoped like hell they would. You know, as long as I was at the right house.

She had to be home by now. Vampires were so fast, that she had to have run this in a day, if she was on foot. Even in a car, she could have made it, and taken one of the early morning ferries over. I'd gotten here midday and drove around waiting for night to fall.

"Hello, the house!" I shouted again. "I'm seeking Morag!"

There was no sign of movement from the house before me. No one in the windows. None of the lights went off, nor did any more go on. It was as though the house was listening. The people inside probably were. Hopefully, they weren't ringing the police.

"My name is Chase. I met her in Edinburgh. According to her, we are bonded," I shouted. That was a risk, but I was really hoping not to die. Or even come close to death.

A hand went over my mouth and I was dragged backward into the woods surrounding the house. I struggled, kicking my legs, trying to find some traction, but the hand was like a band of steel over my mouth, as was the other across my chest. I let myself go limp. *No sense fighting what you can't see.* My brother's words came back to me.

My captor held me tighter, which didn't seem possible, and kept dragging me. Then I was dropped onto the ground abruptly.

"What are you doing here?" Morag hissed as she looked down at me.

It made me feel good to know that she didn't look much happier than I did. There were times when it was nice to know that you weren't suffering alone. This was one of those times for me, even if it wasn't the most caring thing to admit to.

"Looking for you," I said, curling my legs toward me to me to kick up and leap back onto my feet.

Morag crossed her arms, glaring.

Part of me hoped she'd been impressed by the small

demonstration of my skills. Most men couldn't do a kick up.

"You are quite flexible," she said, her face expressionless.

"Which you well know," I shot back. "And which I would have been happy to demonstrate further, except you ran off."

Her shoulders dropped slightly. "There was nothing more to say, Chase."

"Oh, I'm sorry, were you the only one in the conversation? I kind of thought there were two of us," I growled, feeling my patience strain. "Thanks for the nose, by the way. That was what was missing."

"You're still alive." Morag's words were flat.

And that was my thought, also, but I wasn't going to tell her that. Not yet, anyway.

"You need to talk to me," I insisted.

"About what?"

"About this whole mated, or bonded thing, or whatever."

She grabbed my arm, and it felt as though I'd been grabbed by a steel plate. "You're not going to say another thing about the mating bond."

"What is it? What does it mean? Can you say, No, thanks?" I asked. "And it's too late. I already told the whole house, if there's anyone there."

Morag stared at me, then sighed. "No. You can't refuse it. It just... happens. I don't know the details. It's different for everyone. What I know is that when I met you, my heart began to beat. That's the sign. Did you really tell everyone in my home that we were mates?"

"Something like that, yes. I was trying to avoid being killed."

She rubbed at her chest as she looked at me. "That was smart."

"I wasn't ready to die yet. So this mating thing. What if the other party isn't interested?"

She shrugged. "That usually doesn't happen."

"Are you not interested?"

A silence, and then, "It doesn't matter how I feel about it, Chase. We do not suit. You have been a Hunter your entire life—and I am a vampire. We are foes."

"Don't I get a say in this?" When she'd first told me, I hadn't known what to think. The way I felt when she'd left, however, convinced me that there was something to this, something worth taking the time to explore.

"No," she brushed past me. "You need to leave, Chase. If I see you here, if you betray this place to your family," she spat out the word, "You will all die."

"Wait a minute," I grabbed at her arm, but she was too quick. My hand met air. Morag zoomed ahead of me. "Don't do that zipadeedoodah super-fast shit. I came here to talk with you," I yelled at her retreating back.

"There's nothing to say," she called over her shoulder. Then she was gone from my line of sight.

"Fucking zipadeedoodah shit," I muttered, breaking into a run. I'd been running distances since I was young, and we weren't far from the house. When I got back to the drive, the house was still silent, with lights still on. I noted they were the same ones that had been on when I'd driven up. My motorcycle was where I'd left it.

"I'm not leaving," I shouted. "All of you! Morag's clan! Coven! Whatever! I'm here because Morag felt her heart beat when we met. Now she doesn't want to see me. I'm not leaving!"

What I would do if an army of vampires came out was farther along than I'd thought, but I'd take things as they came. I planted my feet and waited.

CHAPTER ELEVEN

Morag

I leaned against the large wooden door, feeling my heart racing. Chase was nervous, and he knew what he was doing was extremely dangerous, but he wasn't backing down.

He was very brave. Stupid, but brave.

"Morag, we can't have him shouting the place down," Collum said. Isabeau was at his side, and the rest of the coven gathered round. "Why is it you won't see him?"

"Because we have a difference of opinion," I said, not wanting to tell them the truth. Then I was angry at myself—why should I protect him?

Because he was my mate.

"And?" Lyall, mated to Clara, crossed his arms and glared at me. "There's not a one of us here who didn't have some troubles in the beginning. That's par for the course when one of the pair is a human."

Clara nodded, and I could see the rest of my coven nodding with her. Damn them. I sighed.

"He's a Hunter."

"What?" Charlotte gasped.

"And you let him come here?" Angus, who was mated to Kyla, demanded as he put an arm around Kyla.

"We'll just have to get rid of him," Margaret said. Her mate, Devon, nodded, and started toward the door.

"Wait!" I held up a hand. "He is a Hunter, but... I believe we met while he was in the midst of... of a crisis of faith."

"A what? Not that it matters," Talbot, Charlotte's mate, said, his face and tone full of disbelief. "Are you making excuses for him?"

"No! Yes! I don't know!" I threw up my hands.

"Do you like him?" Isabeau asked. "Before he told you he was a Hunter, did you like him?"

Her simple question shattered me. "Yes. I did."

"Then you need to talk to him. Because Collum is right. He can't be up here, carrying on and yelling. We're fairly remote, but eventually someone will notice." Isabeau made a face. Even now, the fact that Mull was several small towns on a small island were still too small for her. She was constantly astounded at the way gossip spread.

"Not if we shut him up now," Talbot said.

"No!" I shouted. "No. No one lays a hand on him. If you do, I will take it as a personal affront."

"This is the safety of all of us," Kyla said softly.

"This is Morag's mate," Collum said. "So it is on Morag to manage. We'll let you handle this, but handle this doesn't mean leaving him to shout down the hills in our drive," he gestured at the door behind me.

Chase was yelling something, but I couldn't pay attention because for the first time in decades, I wasn't sure what to do. I knew I didn't want him dead. I wasn't going to kill him, and my coven sure as hell wasn't laying one finger on him.

Which still left me with being the one who had to die. Which sucked, as far as choices went. But I couldn't bear to feel this heartbeat for however many years Chase had left.

"I'll deal with it. I'm going to bring him inside, after I get rid of his knives."

"He has knives?" Isabeau asked.

"That's how I figured out what he was," I said, opening the door. "They're silver."

A shudder ran round the room.

"Exactly," I said. I leaned against the door, feeling more tired than I'd felt in a long time. "Chase?" I stuck my head out. "Please come inside. Leave the knives outside."

I could see him stop shouting, unsure. He looked at me for a moment, and then nodded. He pulled the knives from his inner pocket, dropped them on the ground, and walked toward the door. He was careful, moving like a predator. Like a Hunter.

Like me.

He stepped into the light, and I could feel the reaction of my coven through their quiet hisses. "This is my family," I said. "They know."

He nodded again. "I wouldn't expect you to hide it."

The men moved in front of the women, even though every woman in my coven could have kicked Chase's ass. It was a leftover trait from their human lives.

"And now, they are all going to leave," I said, glaring at my coven. "Because you and I need to talk without an audience."

"Are you sure?" Collum leaned in. "I am happy to stay."

I didn't soften my glare. "I am, Collum, thank you."

"Like we can't hear you," Devon muttered.

I gave him the stink eye. Not really the time.

Collum glanced behind him at the rest of the coven who were tensed and waiting. He nodded once, and I saw everyone ease up a little. They turned and headed out of the foyer.

Collum was the last to go. He directed his words at Chase. "It is only because Morag speaks for you that you come into my home. It is due to her alone that I leave you here. If you attempt to harm her, I will end you." His voice was cold, and resolute, and I realized there was something else going on.

Of course. The recent raid. I was right. We did know

the woman Chase described. Dear Lord. Although the Lord didn't have much to do with raids in any manner that was positive. Usually just the opposite.

Chase nodded. "I understand."

Collum looked at him for a long moment. "Good. I'm glad to hear it." Without looking at me, Collum left.

It was only Chase and me in the foyer. He looked at me. "They love you."

"Of course they do. We're all here by choice."

"That sounds nice—a family you can choose."

"Is that your excuse?" I asked. "You didn't have a choice?"

"No," he said immediately. "I never had a choice. I'm going to have to deal with—well, it doesn't matter. But I wasn't supposed to go to Edinburgh, and I'm already in the shit for that. I've never once, once been asked what I want."

I feel myself wavering. When I became a vampire, I was given a choice. When I was turned, women didn't have many choices. Being a vampire gave me a lot of choices, and autonomy—and I recognized the place where Chase found himself.

But he was a Hunter, and he'd killed my kind. There was no getting around that.

"I understand. But you need to leave. We're not going to work," I said, and I couldn't keep the sadness from my voice. The thought of him leaving, after the way I'd felt when I left him in Edinburgh, tore at my soul. The ache in my heart nearly made me cry out.

"There's a way to work this out, Morag," he pleaded.

"Do you love me?" I asked. I wanted to see what he'd say.

"After only a couple of days? No. I'd like to have the chance to find out, since we're supposed to be together. Wouldn't you?"

Damn him. I had to give him kudos for the honesty. "Of course I would. But I can't get past your past."

"You think it's easy for me?" Chase ran his hands through his hair, obviously in frustration. His hair stood up even more on end than normal. "You're everything I've ever been told is evil. My whole life has been protecting people from you."

"Is that really what you think?" I asked.

"I don't know," he rubbed his neck. "Last week, maybe. Not fully. Not after I grew up. But after seeing my dad, and brothers? I wonder if it's just a way to be..." he stopped and then took a breath. "I wonder if it's just a way to be a killer and call it something else."

My heart, feeling his heart speed up, broke a little for him. None of this changed anything. "You need to leave," I said.

"Please don't do this," Chase said quietly.

"I have to," I said. "It's not going to work." *I'm not going to kill you, and I can't die if you're still here,* I thought.

He looked at me, and I could feel that he was ready to argue. Something in my face must have convinced him that arguing wouldn't do anything.

"You won't even let us try." Chase's voice was flat.

I crossed my arms.

He stepped close to me, leaning down to kiss me on the cheek. "I'm really sorry about that," Chase whispered into my hair. "I'm really sorry. I would have liked to have been with you."

Then he turned and walked out the door, closing it quietly behind him.

CHAPTER TWELVE

Chase

The tears gathered in my eyes as I climbed onto my motorcycle. I hadn't cried since I was a kid, and my dad whipped me for bungling something. The feeling of loss was overwhelming.

Checking the ferry schedule, I realized I wasn't going to be able to get off the island until tomorrow.

"Fuck," I swore.

There weren't many hotels, but I found a bed-and-breakfast about twenty minutes away with a room, and headed off to a night where I knew I wouldn't sleep. All my life, I'd never even thought about love, because it just didn't have a place in my world. I didn't want kids, after growing up with my dad.

But now, I'd met someone, and leaving her hurt. This was what love could be. I hadn't lied to her—I didn't love her now, only a few days after meeting her. I could have. I saw that clearly. I could have.

She'd said no.

The bed-and-breakfast was next to a pub. After I checked in, I went down to get something to eat. When I came into the pub, there were only a few patrons seated at a few tables around the place. I sat at the bar, not wanting any to have to deal with any more interaction than a bartender.

"What'll you have?" The bartender met my eye.

I pointed at the tap with the stout label, and he nodded. "And a glass of Laphroaig, neat," I added. Whiskey was also necessary tonight.

He set a menu in front of me, which I stared at blankly.

My heart ached, and quite simply, I needed to dull it for the night. I could feel something within me hurting at the thought that I'd never see Morag again.

It wasn't just that—it was that there was no chance to be with someone who was chosen to be something to me.

Damn it.

I ordered a steak, and drank my beer, then sipped at my whiskey. Why wouldn't she give me—give us—a chance?

How long would this hurt like this? I'd never experienced anything like it. It was as though I'd gotten the worst ass kicking of my life, and it wasn't going away. I felt worse than when I'd first gotten here.

I ate the food when it was placed in front of me. I had another beer, and another whiskey. There was nothing here for me, nothing at all. After settling the bill, I went back to my room.

Tomorrow, I'd have to go home.

Sleep took a long time coming, and when I woke, I didn't feel any better. I checked the ferry schedule again and got a ticket.

As the ferry left the Isle of Mull, I watched from the back of the boat as the island got smaller. I felt like I was leaving a piece of me behind.

And that really sucked.

I drove home, pushing the motorcycle to unsafe speeds on the quiet roads. We lived outside of the village of Tynehall, which was east of Edinburgh. I drove all day, and it was late afternoon when I went through the village.

Outside the village limits, I stopped, gathering myself. I hadn't been thinking about dealing with my family. There was no avoiding them now. I'd go home, tell them I was leaving, and go... I didn't know where.

How could I feel this way after only two days? Okay, three, if you counted today. But my life had changed. It had changed even before I met Morag. Meeting her had solidified things for me, though. There was no way I could go back to being a Hunter.

Because side by side, my family was far worse. Had Morag walked into our home the way I'd strolled into Lochdon House, she would have been dead on the floor and turning to ash in under sixty seconds. They wouldn't have allowed her to speak, to be alone with me, or to live.

And yet, my family saw Morag as violent predators.

When we'd been the ones out hunting last week.

Shame washed over me again. I hoped that the women who had knocked me down and ran with the kids got away. I hoped no one in our family had caught them. I hoped they made it to safety.

There was no putting it off. While I wasn't sure what kind of life I'd have after tomorrow, I needed to close the door on this one.

It was close to dusk when I turned down the lane to our house. Everything was quiet and still. That was odd—normally, my dad or my brothers would be out practicing. Either with guns, or arrows, or knives—there was always something to get better at killing with.

I parked my motorcycle and went into the house. Mom wasn't in the kitchen.

"Hello?" I called out. All the various vehicles were in the garage, so everyone was home. "Hello?"

We had a barn where we practiced hand to hand fighting, and I went out the back door and toward it. I could see that there was a light on somewhere in the barn. Pulling back the door, I shouted in, "Hello? Where is everyone?"

My father appeared out of the darkness. The main floor of the barn was lit with a few candles. Both of my brothers, Brayden and Cole, stood behind him. They all gazed at me with hard, unforgiving expressions.

"You've finally come back," Dad said.

"Yes. I told you I needed some time," I said.

"Some time," Dad turned to look at Brayden. "He needed some time."

Brayden snickered.

"Did ya sort it all out, Chase?" Dad asked, his voice full of false concern. "Everything all better?"

"No, as a matter of fact, it's not," I said. "That's why I came home."

"To what? Apologize?"

"For what?" I asked.

"For being a bloody great failure. Again. For letting the unholy devils and their demon spawn get away," Dad said conversationally. "It's time we talk about how you're going to fix this, Chase."

"One of them hit me, and they were faster than I was. And there's nothing to fix."

"Excuses, ya see," Dad turned to Cole this time. "Plenty of 'em."

"Sounds like it," Cole said, crossing his arms.

"Yeah, those don't work around here," Dad looked back at me. "I thought I'd trained you better than that."

"How you trained me doesn't matter," I said, getting impatient. "I came to tell you that I'm done."

"Done?" Dad asked. He was surprised.

"This is not the life I want."

"Well, isn't that nice? We raise ya up, try to give ya a

good set of morals, food in the belly, a roof over your head, and a calling. And that's not enough?"

"Since when do we try to kill children?" I asked.

"They're not children," Dad's voice was low and deadly. "They're smaller versions of their elders. That's all."

"You're wrong," I said.

There was silence in the barn, and I heard a gasp. My mom. She must be in the shadows somewhere.

Of course she was. Because where else would she be?

"No, boy, I'm not. And it seems you need to learn that lesson again." He crossed his arms and nodded.

Brayden and Cole rushed me, and while it took me off guard, I crouched down, ready to take them from the middle. Brayden hit me on my left, and I swung at him, catching him in the side of his head.

Then I felt a hard, solid object hit me right where Dad had lashed me. I stumbled, and Brayden took advantage of my stumble to punch me in the face.

Everything went dark. My last thought was, Morag....

~

I opened my eyes, and I was tied to a chair. Dad, Brayden, and Cole were standing in a semi-circle around me.

"What the fuck?" I spat out.

"Such language, with his family of all things," Dad said. "We were going to have a nice talk with ya, Chase. An intervention, I've heard it called. To talk about why ya can't seem to get the hang of this calling. Why ya hesitate. Why ya let the hell spawn get away at our last raid. We were going to give ya a chance. To repent and make things right. Weren't we, boys?"

My brothers nodded.

"But then, we realized the truth. Ya were never going to take advantage of the gift of being born to this life, this calling. And that was before we found out what happened after the raid."

Cole spat at my feet.

"What happened after the raid?" I asked.

"Well, if ya recall, we were to meet up at the house of Jeffrey. To celebrate, to go over things. And your brothers and I were there, even if you weren't. The sight that greeted us," he closed his eyes and crossed himself.

Brayden and Cole crossed themselves as well.

"One of the demon spawn—no doubt one you let get away—came back. And killed all of those there. All of them, Chase!" Dad was shouting now. "Every single life, gone! Torn to bits, arms and legs and heads not in their proper place," he stopped, his voice breaking as his head dropped down.

Then Dad looked me in the eyes. "And that's when we realized an intervention isn't what's needed."

"What's needed?" I was incredulous. "You're sitting here with your one of your sons tied to a chair, after you've beat the hell out of him. You're angry that the people we've been killing are fighting back. As if their deaths don't matter to them like ours do to us? What's needed is the doctor, to check your mental state, you insane bastard!"

"See, it breaks my heart to hear ya speak so. To say nothing of your mother. She's not stopped crying since ya left. But what's worse is that I see it's of no use. You are set on the path of evil."

"Do you hear yourself?" I asked. "The path of evil? I'm your son, and I don't agree with you. That's it. I'll leave, Dad. I'll leave, never tell anyone about you, and you can forget all about me."

Dad shook his head. "No, that's not going to work, Chase. Sad as it is for me to say, you need to be cleansed. You can't go out into the world spreading all your filth."

"Dad, you need to stop this."

Brayden came closer, Cole right behind him. "No, you need to shut your mouth," he said. Brayden punched me on side of the head, then Cole hit me on the other.

If I didn't die, I was going to really need a cat scan. The number of punches to the head were getting ridiculous.

The last thing I saw was my dad standing silently behind them, arms crossed, watching with approval.

CHAPTER THIRTEEN

Morag

I sat up straight. I'd just woken, but something had jerked me upright. It was if someone had poked at me, forcing me awake. My heart exploded in a burst of pain.

After I sent Chase away, I went to my room, and locked my door. I didn't come out the rest of the evening, even as I knew my coven was worried. Not just about me, but what would this guy who was a Hunter do? Mostly about me, though. I could feel their concern. Isabeau had come in and insisted I eat, emptying a bag of blood into a glass and sitting with me until I drank it.

There was concern not only because of me, but because of Fenella. She was the silvery-blond haired vampire Chase had mentioned. Collum told me that

Harry, one of the members of her coven, one of Fenella's children, had come to see him Friday evening.

While I was rolling around naked with Chase, Harry was telling the tale of watching his entire coven meet the sun. They'd been tortured, as Chase had told me. Fenella had spoken to Harry with her mind, letting him know all of what happened.

And the next night, after he rose, Harry killed them all. I wondered if that included Chase's family. Seeing what they'd done to Chase, I couldn't feel any sympathy for them. They were monsters.

But Chase wasn't. He'd refused to harm the children, and the women with them. He'd refused to go hunting them.

Harry had left that evening, off to America to see a former coven mate of Collum's. Miles, who'd settled in Lake Tahoe. Where maybe he could get away from the Hunters. I hoped he'd find some peace.

Even though I was overcome with guilt about being with someone who'd been part of the horrific raid, I didn't want Chase to die. I slept the next day as restlessly as I'd been sleeping since I'd met Chase. I could feel his heartbeat through mine, although fainter, and it reminded me of what I had before me. When the sun went down, I woke, but I didn't get up right away. Because what was there to get up for? I was just going to have to find a way to say goodbye to my coven and sneak away without any of them, particularly Collum, figuring out what I was up to.

Until this moment. The echo of something dread-fully wrong rang in my mind.

"Hello?" I said softly into the room, even as I knew no one would answer.

What was it? What had woken me up? I listened so hard it made my head hurt.

"Chase?" I asked, and got no answer from my empty room. I stood up, throwing off the blankets and putting on clothes. We all had various sleeping arrangements for when it was time for us to escape the sun. I'd turned a large storage area into my sleeping room. Collum had a bed under his bed, which was freaky as hell to me, but to each their own. Most of us enjoyed the opportunity to sleep in a bed in a windowless room. Old houses had plenty of those.

I hurried through getting myself together, not even stopping to take a shower. Something was wrong. I left my room and went straight to the large dining room. Not that we ate, but it was a central gathering place. Everyone made their way there once they got up, and then people tended to disburse from there. The couple that took care of things during the day, Constance, and her husband Martin, left at dark, so it was just us. The balance of coordinated togetherness and time away from one another was part of what made our coven successful.

When I came into the dining room, Kyla, Talbot, and Charlotte were sitting at the table, reading and looking over their laptops.

"Are you all right?" Kyla asked. "You look off."

"I am," I said, "I don't know why. I mean, outside of everything," I waved a hand to encompass Chase, the fact that he was a Hunter, the fact that our community had been attacked. "I woke up hearing feeling like something was wrong. Like, life or death wrong."

Talbot and Charlotte looked at one another meaningfully.

"What?" I demanded.

"Did you share blood with the Hunter?" Kyla was the one who spoke again.

"No," I said.

"How have you been feeling since he left?" Charlotte asked.

"Like shit," I said. "Absolute shit. I hurt."

"It's your mate," Talbot said with a huff. "He's in distress, somehow."

"But you sent him away." Kyla looked at me thoughtfully.

"Not to be in pain, or die!" I cried.

The three of them were all about the sharing of looks now.

"What?" I shouted.

Talbot sighed. "It seems there is no choice. This is your mate, Morag. You've already strongly connected with him, even without blood. I'm assuming you slept with him?"

"Repeatedly," I muttered. I hated this.

Kyla snickered. "Well, there are more ways than blood to connect."

"What do I do?" I asked.

"Have you heard anything that makes you think it's him specifically?" Charlotte asked.

I shook my head. "No, other than a gut instinct."

"Isabel heard Collum," Kyla said thoughtfully.

Isabeau, when she'd still been human, had heard Collum as he was being attacked. She'd run to him. "They shared blood," I said.

"Every mating bond is different," Charlotte said.

Talbot said, "As crappy as this will sound, you need to wait. If you don't know where he is—"

I cut him off. "I don't have any idea where he lives. I'm guessing the Hunter families don't have a sign announcing where they live ."

"No, that would make sense. You know his last name?" This was from Kyla.

"Yes, it's Robson. Chase Robson."

"Then let's look up Robsons. Was he from Edinburgh?"

"No, he came there from wherever it was their evil lair is located," I said, unable to stem my sarcasm.

"We'll look around there, then," Charlotte said, ignoring me.

I walked around the table to lean over Talbot's shoulder as he searched.

Thirty minutes later, we had a list of Robsons who all lived on farms, within a couple of hours of Edinburgh, in more rural areas with no real neighbors. That's what I remembered from Chase's description.

What to do now was the next question, and I hated not being sure.

I also had the uncomfortable realization I owed my entire coven an apology. When I told them that I knew something was wrong, hinting at who might be the reason for my current distress, they didn't question me, didn't give me any grief. Because they knew. They were all mated.

"What's going on?" Isabeau came in with Margaret, Isabeau rubbing her eyes. Collum and Devon were behind them.

"Morag woke up to a bad feeling," Charlotte said.

"It's her mate," Talbot didn't bother to hide his displeasure. "He's in some kind of trouble."

"So what are you doing?" Margaret asked.

"Looking for him, what else?" Talbot grumbled.

Isabeau smiled at me, coming over to put an arm around me. "We'll find him," she said.

"Even when we do, he's still a Hunter." Finding him didn't solve the central problem.

"Well, if you two are mated, then we need to accept that," Collum said. "I don't like it either, but we'll figure something out."

A wave of love for my coven—my chosen family— washed over me. "Thank you," I said. "It's a lot to ask," I began.

"We understand. We can't choose who our mates

are," Collum said. "However, if he joins us, there will be matters which need to be discussed."

"Understood," I said.

"But no more shit from you," Charlotte said. "About old mated people, or any of that other nonsense you like to toss off."

Everyone laughed, even me. I needed the laughter, because my nerves were being shot to pieces. I could normally go in and handle things. That was my role, and I enjoyed it. But this not knowing what was wrong even as I knew something was wrong made me want to tear someone's hair out. Not mine. But someone's.

Whoever it was that was making Chase hurt, or worry, or whatever it was. I'd do more than that, however. I'd tear them limb from limb.

A sharp ache hit my heart, and my hand went to it automatically, rubbing the spot where the ache was. I felt, rather than saw, everyone at the table notice.

But no one said anything, and for that, I was grateful.

While several of my coven mates continued looking for Chase's family, I went outside, to burn off some of my anxiety and run the grounds. When I was upset, it was better for me to get outside, do something physical. I ran the perimeter around the house twice and came back in.

"All is well?" Lyall asked, coming upon me in the hall as I walked back in the door.

"Yes, I—" I stopped. There it was again. The feeling

of impending doom. Sharp and pointed. My hand went to my heart, which sent a wave of pain so strong I leaned forward. It slowed and I was able to step back outside. "No. Can you hear it?" I asked Lyall.

He came to stand beside me. "Are you all right?"

"Not at all. What do you feel?" I made myself stand, and rubbed at my heart.

"You're right," Lyall said, "There is something very wrong."

He walked out into the drive, listening to the night. Lyall was able to sense high emotion in addition to being able to communicate telepathically, so if someone was in pain and close enough, he might be able to sense it. He turned to me, his face troubled. "There is something on the isle that doesn't belong," he said.

"What do you mean? Is it Chase?"

"I can't tell, but something's not right."

"Something as in, We need to go see what it is sort of something?" I asked. Sometimes Lyall wasn't very specific. Although in fairness, we didn't really have many issues on Mull. It was quiet, and peaceful. Most of the time.

"Yes," he said.

We walked back into the house to tell Collum. When Lyall explained, Collum said, "We do need to see what it is that is triggering Lyall's senses. Only five of us should go, however. Everyone else stays here. That way, we can keep looking for Chase, and no one is left unprotected."

One of the reasons I loved this coven so was the way that Collum made everything a family matter.

"Do you think this connected to what Morag is feeling?" Collum asked Lyall.

"I don't know. The timing is suspicious."

Collum nodded. "Agreed. Well, we'll know soon enough."

"I'm going," I said.

"As if I could stop you," Collum rolled his eyes. "I think Margaret, Talbot, and Lyall should also go, in addition to you and I."

There was no dissent, and within minutes, the five of us were out of the house and running south through the woods. Lyall stopped and closed his eyes.

"We're going the right way," he said.

We continued south.

"We're almost at the end of the island," Margaret said.

"This is the place," Lyall said. He stopped, looking out over the hills, which led down to the sea. "It's at the abbey."

Iona Abbey was just across the water on the Isle of Iona. It was an old Christian site, and now a historical site. It was also only open during the day, so anyone there right now wasn't supposed to be.

And that meant no ferry. Damn it.

"Great, we have to swim," Margaret said, echoing my thoughts. "That was not on my to-do list this evening."

"Damn it," I said out loud.

"We can go back," Collum looked at me.

"No, we need to see what it is. If it's strong enough to bother Lyall, it's nothing good."

"Sensible, even as I am not looking forward to the swim either," Talbot said.

We all looked at one another and then ran to the edge of the cliff. Almost as one, we dived in. We didn't need to breath, so the long swim wasn't a problem. The current was strong, but not strong enough to sweep any of us away. All I could think was I'd never get the smell out. Something bumped into me, and I automatically punched at it. Nothing else came close to me the rest of the swim. Thank God. I had enough to worry about. I was hoping that whatever waited for us on Iona wasn't anything to do with me or Chase. That Lyall's bad feeling and my waking up feeling like the world had just gone wrong were two separate events.

Another part of me hoped that this was something to do with me or Chase. I wanted to see him again. Even if for just a moment.

As we came out onto the small strip of sand, we made our way up the cliff, and onto the grounds of the abbey. Thank heavens for fast healing. The rocks were sharp, and scraped at my hands. As we reached the top, we stopped to look around.

The moon was full. Iona Abbey rose like a dark shadow in the night, and I saw a flicker around the front of the abbey itself.

"There," I said, pointing.

The five of us took off running silently, making our way to the abbey. As we came closer, I could see that the flicker was actually a fire.

"Yeah, definitely not supposed to be here," Talbot said.

I sighed. As a place of importance to history, there were sometimes nuts who hid on the island and tried to do whatever it was nuts did.

"Great," Margaret said.

"Wait—" I threw out my arms, stopping everyone from taking another step. My heart was beating, as it had been since I'd met Chase.

Right now, however, it was stronger, and it had just sped up.

"Look," I hissed, pointing at the people around the fire.

CHAPTER FOURTEEN

Chase

I watched my father and brothers warily. "Why are we here?" I asked again, not really expecting an answer. I'd been asking ever since I woke up in the back of one of the vans and we were barreling across Scotland. No one had given me an answer. Now we were on a boat, or ferry, or something like that. I could feel the difference from being on the road.

As I was tied hand and foot, I figured that whatever the plan was, it didn't bode well for me. The worst thing, in my opinion, is that I wasn't surprised that my father was treating me like this. Or that my brothers were just going on along with it. Or that I hadn't seen my mother since I'd come home. She'd been in the barn, I was fairly certain. But she wasn't with us now.

What the hell was wrong with my family? Why hadn't I seen this before? Why had I stayed for so long?

Because I was a coward, too afraid to break away. Because I told myself we didn't do that many raids anymore. Because.. because... excuses, as my father would say.

I shook my head to try to clear it. The movement had Cole looking around to glare at me. I closed my eyes and let my head slump. There was no need to give him an excuse to hit me again.

Wherever we were going, we were on a boat. Jesus, what were they up to? I hoped we weren't on Mull.

I'd been planning to tell them the truth—that I felt we were wrong, that I'd met vampires, and unlike us, they hadn't killed first and asked questions later. That maybe we didn't need to live this kind of life.

But they'd beaten the crap out of me *again*, and I realized discussion wasn't possible. In fact, I'd been an idiot to think it could ever happen. Especially not now, as I sat here tied and even more bruised. I wasn't weak, or a pushover, but both of my brothers against me? I didn't have a good chance. I was also really tired of getting my ass kicked this week.

Thankfully, the beating had stopped me from saying anything about Morag and her coven. She may not want to be with me, but I wasn't going to put her or the rest of them in the line of fire from my insane family.

Maybe this was why I'd never felt completely at ease

with my family, or the other Hunters we'd been friendly with.? Maybe this was why I'd always felt like an outsider?

Maybe this was why I'd met Morag, and fate had made us mates? Because I was supposed to meet her, supposed to be able to walk away from the only life I'd ever known.

I felt a resolve rise up. I'd get out of this mess, and I was going back to her. I wouldn't let our pasts get in the way again. Why should we both be miserable—and I'd been miserable since I'd left her, even without the family beatings—when we didn't have to be?

Straightening, I looked around. I needed to find a way to get myself out of this.

Shit.

While I couldn't credit my brothers with critical thinking, they hadn't left anything around that I could use to free myself.

Shit.

I leaned back against the wall of the van, letting my eyes close. Better that they think me asleep, or hurt, or weak. Preferably all three.

There were voices at the window of the van. Dad was talking to someone in a whisper. Were there more Hunters with us? Great.

The van left what I assumed was the ferry—I could feel the bump as we drove off onto land, and again, I wondered where we were. Please don't let it be Mull.

"Still daylight," Brayden said.

"We'll settle in somewhere away from all the tourists," Dad said. "They don't patrol the entire place."

Cole said something, but I couldn't hear him, even as I strained to do so.

My dad grunted, and then the van came to an abrupt stop.

"Where are we? And when are you going to let me go and stop this stupid shit?" I said.

All three of them turned to look at me. Dad came out of the driver's seat to the back where I was tied.

"Shut your mouth. You're a traitor to your kind," he growled.

"What the hell are you talking about?" I got out.

He hit me, and then hit me again, and again. Fuck it all, this shit was old! I could see stars, and then I couldn't see anything at all.

~

When I woke, it was dark. I wasn't in the van anymore, thank God. But I was—I took a moment to take stock of my surroundings. Mother of God. I was tied to a post. My arms were tied over my head, stretching at my shoulders. This would get painful soon. I'd need to manage this, so I could get out of here and find the woman I was meant to be with.

I turned my head. We were out in the middle of nowhere, given the stars. There was a church in front of me, with a large stone cross off to one side.

Jesus, Mary, and Joseph. What the hell? I was tied to a fucking post.

Straining my neck, I could see my dad and brothers and three men I didn't know standing around a small fire they'd made. I let my head fall against the post. No sense in letting them know I was awake.

Carefully, I turned my head to look the other way. I could see buildings around us, but they were all dark. Wherever we were, it was the middle of nowhere. My dad's favorite kind of place. Fewer people to see what crazy shit he was doing.

Why hadn't I left them before? I could kick my own ass right now. But if I'd left before, I wouldn't have met Morag.

I heard them coming closer, so I let my head fall to the post again, feigning unconsciousness.

"Wake up," I heard my dad's voice behind me.

I didn't move.

"Wake him up," he commanded.

A hit in the kidney on my right side made me arch back in pain.

"Awake now, aren't ya?" Dad asked, satisfaction in his voice.

"What the hell is going on?" I growled. "Have you lost your fucking mind?"

There was silence, and then my dad said, "You must have, to be talking to your da that way. That's not how a respectful son speaks to his elders."

"Really? When my elders are repeatedly kicking the shit out of me?" I yelled.

"You're a traitor," Dad's voice was flat and murderously angry. "You're a traitor to your own kind."

"What in the crazy hell are you talking about?" I asked.

"What am I talking about? Boys, he wants to know what I'm talking about," Dad said.

"Who is Morag?" Cole asked. "Because you sure do miss her."

"Yeah, and you're completely fine with her being a *vampire*," Brayden spat out the last word.

A cold shiver of fear ran through me. How did they know? How in the hell did they know?

"Ya talk a lot when you're down for the count. Like the weakling you are. We know all about Morag, the demon you've been with. You're a traitor to your kind, Chase, and for that, you have to pay," Dad said.

"Did you tell them where everyone was going to be?" Cole got in my face. "When everyone was at Jeffrey's? Did you tell them, so some fucking vampire could go and kill them?"

"I didn't even know we were supposed to go there until you told me," I said, letting my head fall against the post.

"Sure," Brayden said. "And you didn't fuck a vampire, either."

"No, that part is true. I did. More than once. She's incredible." Fuck all of them. If I was going to die, and it

was possible that was the grand plan, I was going out
with no regrets in terms of Morag.

"Where is she?" Dad said in a low, dangerous voice.
"Tell us where to find the demon spawn."

"No," I said. "Do what you like to me. I'm not telling
you shit."

"We know she's on Mull," Brayden said with great
satisfaction. "Your motorcycle has a GPS tracker."

No. No, no no.

"But we couldn't get the specific location," Dad said.
"You'll give us that now."

"Like hell. You can fuck right off. All of you. All six
of you! Yeah, I saw, six on one! Gearing up for some
more torture? Like you did the other night?" I was
shouting now, not caring that I was probably signing
my own death notice.

"You're taken by the devil," Dad sighed. "There's no
help for ya. But you must pay. Boys," he said to my
brothers, and stepped back. "In this holy place, let us
see if we can't help your fallen brother find his way to
God one last time."

I wondered where the three men I'd seen around
the fire were. They weren't there anymore. Then I heard
the whistle of a whip.

I bent my head to grab my tee shirt with my teeth. I
wanted something in my mouth so I didn't bite my
tongue. I'd seen people who bit their tongues off being
thrashed. The first lash of the whip seared across my
already tender back

Brayden said viciously, "You think you're bound somehow to one of these evil undead bitches?"

Crack!

I bit down on my tee shirt. I was horrified I'd blurted out this much to them while unconscious.

"You think you can turn your back on us? This is who you are," Cole's voice was in my ear.

Crack!

I jumped again. Then another, and another. My fingers dug into the wood of the post I leaned against, my teeth grinding together. I was not going to make a sound. Not in front of these madmen. Never again.

Crack! Crack! Crack!

As I worked to keep myself calm and still, because fuck these guys, the lashing stopped.

Cole said, "I have an idea." Then he spoke louder, for my benefit. "You think your blood is so fucking precious? Too good for the likes of us? Well, let's see what happens when we spill your blood for her."

My shoulder was grabbed, and he yanked me, making my arms scream in pain, spinning me around. I saw him standing in front of me, holding a knife with a demented grin on his face. Brayden stood next to him, whip held down at his side. Watching.

And off in the distance, my father. Arms crossed, no expression on his face. Nothing. We might as well have been out mowing the fields, for all the emotion he showed.

"She won't come. There's no bond anymore," I let

my head fall forward. "She sent me away." I hated to admit that.

"That may be," Cole said, still grinning. "But things change when there's blood involved, don't they?"

I didn't answer. There was nothing to say. If I saw her again, it would be because somehow I escaped, and I went to her.

Then Cole leaned forward, and sliced my chest with the knife, satisfaction showing in his face when my blood began to spill.

CHAPTER FIFTEEN

Morag

*W*e all watched, staying perfectly still, as three men detached themselves from the fire. They stopped to go into the back of one of the two vans parked a short distance away and re-emerged carrying bows. They trotted off into some of the smaller ruins of outbuildings.

"Tipped with silver, no doubt," Talbot muttered.

"Of course it's a trap," Margaret snapped impatiently, although no one had said anything about a trap. "They use the same tired playbook."

"And sometimes they succeed," Collum said quietly. "Morag, are you sure you want to do this?"

"I can't let him die," I said.

"Even if you won't see him again?"

"I can't let him die," I repeated. He had to live. One of us had to.

There was a silence, then Collum spoke. "Very well. Margaret, can you handle the snipers?"

Margaret sniffed, apparently offended Collum even had to ask.

"Excellent." I could tell that Collum was smiling. "Lyall, you go with her. Just in case one of them gets lucky," he added, stilling any protest from Margaret. "I think it will really add the right amount of insult to injury to get taken down by a vampire woman."

"Nice," Talbot said.

"Does it need to be tidy?" Margaret asked.

I almost laughed, but that would have been too loud. We conversed quietly enough that the humans couldn't hear us, but I was sure they'd hear me laughing.

"No. Do what you need to," Collum said, dismissing the lives of the snipers in the ruins.

They deserved it. They were lying in wait to kill us.

"Talbot, Morag and I will rescue Chase, well, you'll do it, Morag," Collum said. "Talbot and I will take care of the other three."

"I think those are his father and brothers," I said.

"And they call us animals?" Margaret asked.

"Later," Collum said. His hand reached out suddenly and grabbed me, stopping me. He'd seen it before I had.

They began to whip Chase. Again. The bastards.

And then the one brother drew a knife across Chase's chest.

Collum held me, even as I struggled against him. "No, Morag! We go in together, and together, we'll save him." His grip tightened, and finally, I was able to master myself.

"Here, little vampire," the brother holding the knife called out into the night. "Come and get your bitch."

I would kill him for that.

"Are you calm?" Collum's voice was in my ear.

"No, but yes," I said.

His arm released me. I breathed in, and I could smell the blood of my mate. Of Chase. Holy hell, did he smell delicious.

"Try not to bite first, Morag," Margaret said. "It's rescue, then bite."

I glared as she snickered.

"Are we clear?" Collum asked.

Everyone nodded. "Then you two get going," he said to Margaret and Lyall.

They sped off into the dark.

"Let's give them a minute to take out the snipers," Collum said.

I nodded even as I kept my eyes on Chase. His head had fallen forward, and the blood stained his shirt, dark and foreboding, even by the dim light of the fire.

If he died... I would kill all of them slowly.

"He's not going to die," Collum said. "The bleeding has already slowed."

"You're sure?"

He nodded. "You're not thinking clearly. It's under-standable, but you need to be able to focus, not lose your head. Can you do that?"

"Yes," I said.

"If I think you can't, I'll take care of it," he warned.

"I understand," I said, my teeth grinding together. Which sucked when my fangs were out.

"Stop stressing so hard," Talbot said. "You know we're going to get him."

"We know it's hard to watch," Collum added.

Before us, both of the men I assumed were Chase's brothers were yelling into the dark, their voices taunting and jeering. They were assholes who needed to die merely for being sadistic assholes. But the guy standing back, his arms crossed—Chase's father.

This was on him. This was all his show. He hated my kind so much he'd sacrifice his son. He needed to die slowly.

I took a breath. It wasn't my decision. This needed to be Chase's decision. If we were going to be together, there couldn't be the death of his fam—I stopped myself. Since when had I started to think we could be together? When had I moved on from saving him and going off to die alone?

Somewhere between when I sent him away and now, I guessed.

Watching him, feeling his heart race, feeling his fear, and worry, and pain, and hearing him tell his family to fuck off, protecting me, protecting us—something in me had shifted.

If we all made it out of this, I was going to ask him to give us a chance. He might not want to, after I kicked him to the curb, and he got the shit kicked out of him again by these self-righteous assholes.

He looked terrible. A wave of guilt rushed over me. I'd sent him away, and right into their hands.

A sudden noise made all three of us turn toward the ruins. I doubted the humans heard it, but I was fairly certain one sniper was gone.

I heard another sound that was definitely the death gurgle of a man, and then a third.

"Well, that's taken care of," Collum said with satisfaction. "I hope they made them eat their silver fucking arrows." He didn't swear much, but the with death of Fenella's coven, and my little adventure, everyone was on edge.

"Then let's go," I said.

"You get Chase. We'll handle the others."

"Don't kill them yet," I said.

"Why not?" Talbot and Collum both looked at me.

"Let Chase decide," I said. I knew it wouldn't be a popular thing, but this was his family. He needed to have a say.

Collum inhaled. "I make no promises. We'll hold off on killing them... at least not right away. Are we ready?"

Talbot and I nodded.

"Go," Collum whispered.

The three of us shot out of our hiding spot in the shadows. The two brothers were still mocking and taunting Chase, and though it hurt my feelings, I bypassed them to get around to the other side of the post Chase was tied to. His hands were over his head. I didn't know how long he'd been there, but if it had been any length of time, his arms were going to be mush.

I gave the rope that held his arms up a yank. As it broke free, Chase collapsed to the ground. I moved around the post and picked him up, slinging him over one shoulder.

"Hey, you fucking bitch! Put him down!" I heard of the men roar.

Another tried to join in, but his voice cut off abruptly.

I looked over to my right, and I could see that all three men were being held—the father by Margaret, and the brothers by Collum and Lyall. Obviously the sniper detail was done. I grinned.

Talbot came over to me. "You wanted them alive? There they are," he gestured.

I gently lowered Chase to the ground. "Can you stand?" I asked.

"Abso-fucking-lutely," he said.

He was pissed. It wasn't just fear that had been making his heart beat. He was angry. My heart swelled with pride at my mate. He was a fighter, whatever else he was. And that was no small thing.

I let him use my arm to stand, and he turned to look at his family.

"What do you want to do with them?" I asked.

"They tortured and massacred the vampires at our last raid. They tortured me. They treat everyone who is not with them as not only an enemy, but someone to be torn to shreds." His voice was full of bitter anger.

"They all deserved to die," the father said.

"And you call us animals?" Margaret snorted as she kicked the father in the back. I hope his kidneys were bleeding. "Look what you did. You didn't get them all. We heard. All vampires have heard." Her voice dripped with menace.

"There were children in that coven," Collum said.

The man Collum was holding laughed. "Yeah, and they all cried out for their precious Fenella. Not so fierce when the humans fight back, are ya?"

Collum struck him in the face, and the man's head hung down as blood dripped from somewhere on his face.

"We could say the same thing," Talbot stepped close, and the man held by Lyall flinched. "When it's twenty to one, you're all pretty brave."

"If you do this, it will be your soul," the father spoke to Chase, his eyes dark and glittering in the light of the fire. "Ya will be damned forever."

"I already am," Chase said. "You've put blood on my hands that will never wash off."

"And ya think bedding down with this harpy," the

father indicated me, "Will somehow make it all better?" He started to laugh and then stopped as Margaret hit him in the face.

"Morag has asked that you be allowed to speak for them," Collum said to Chase.

"You're all going to die," one of the brothers spat.

"From what?" Talbot crossed his arms. "From your snipers' arrows? No, I don't think so. They're already rotting in the grass. Try again."

Both of the brothers' eyes widened, and their heads turned toward their father. He saw it and stared defiantly at us. "If you do not save us, and strike them all down, you're cursed, Chase. Cursed with immortal darkness. There will never be light for you again. You will—"

His words stopped as Chase, who'd pushed away from me while his father was speaking, punched his father in the face.

"Shut up, you obnoxious windbag," Chase said. "I'm tired of your shit."

"Well?" Margaret demanded. "What do you want to do with them? We have things to do." She gave the father a shake. I could swear I heard his teeth rattle and I grinned at her.

She grinned back.

Chase looked down, and I could feel his indecision. They were, after all, his family.

"Will you go from here and leave us in peace?" Chase asked his father finally.

The man spat at Chase's feet. "Never. I will return, and hunt you and your bitch and all this filth down."

Chase looked at Collum. "The only reason the kids got away was because one of the women with them knocked me on my ass."

"Lot of that going around, apparently," Margaret said.

I glared. I wasn't sure Chase heard her, because he continued speaking. "They were fine with me killing kids. They weren't willing to do it themselves, but they wanted me to do it. Kids," he glared at his brothers. "Although I guess they were too busy with the torture to have time to off a couple of kids."

"And they got away," one of the brothers said.

"Not because of anything you did," Chase shot back. "Had it been up to you, they would be dead like the rest."

"They killed the Hunters that were with us!" The other brother howled.

"You wouldn't consider that self-defense?" Chase asked.

I wanted so badly to smack the heads off these arrogant killers. But this was Chase's family, and he had to drive this. To whatever conclusion it took.

His father lifted his head and stared defiantly. "No. I do not. These things are immoral, and unnatural, and if you turn your back on your family, on all that is good and decent, you'll regret it forever."

Chase stared at his father for what seemed like a

long time. The vampires were fine—we were used to long periods of stillness.

His father and brothers, however, were getting twitchy and anxious.

"You need to pay," Chase said slowly. "You have harmed many, and you would continue to harm me, your own son. You would have killed me."

"What do you want to do?" I asked.

"Kill them." Chase's voice was flat.

"No!" shouted one brother.

"You bastard!" screamed the other.

Both struggled against their captors. I ignored it. They weren't going anywhere.

Chase's father just stared at him, not saying a word.

"Are you sure?" Collum asked.

"Yes. You're not safe from them. It's not just that I'm not safe—no one here is," Chase said.

"Very well," Collum said.

The father spoke. "You will burn in hell for this, Chase."

Chase didn't blink. "I already am."

I put a hand on his arm. "They'll take care of this, quickly," I said. "You don't have to stay."

"That's right, run away, you fucking coward!" That was from one of his brothers.

"Wow," I said. "I guess it's better than begging."

"We don't beg," the brother said, hearing me.

"Good thing we don't kill like you do," I retorted. "Chase, we can leave."

Chase shook his head. "No, I need to stay. I've looked away for far too long, Morag. Had I stopped looking away years ago... well, a lot more people would be alive."

"Traitor," his father said.

I had to give it to Chase's dad. He wasn't giving an inch.

"Go ahead," Chase said to Collum.

Collum nodded, and almost as one, Margaret, Collum and Lyall twisted the heads of the men in front of them.

Without any fanfare it was done. Six men lay dead around the abbey.

Chase turned to me. "What will we do with the bodies?"

"Who will miss them?" Collum came to where we stood together.

"My mother. The other three, I don't know," Chase shrugged. "I didn't know them."

"Then we toss them over the cliff," Margaret had joined us.

Everyone looked to Chase. He nodded.

Margaret, Lyall, Collum, and Talbot managed to get all six men to the edge of the cliff. Then one at a time, the dead men went over. It was done quickly, and silently. Chase had his hands clasped together in front of him. His heart was beating wildly, and his hands were clasped tightly.

"What will happen when they're found?" Chase

asked no one in particular.

"Their vans are here. They'll be chalked up to people who come here for strange reasons and come to harm," Collum said. His voice was gentler.

Chase nodded.

"We need to go back to the house," Collum said to me. "You both will need to stay here. At least until tomorrow."

"But the daylight—" Chase began.

I put a hand on his arm. "We'll be fine, Collum," I said.

"Then we'll see you both tomorrow. I'll let the CCCCs know to expect Chase." With a nod, Collum, Margaret, Talbot and Lyall turned away, heading toward a less rocky section of the cliff. Then they dived off it.

"Did they just dive into the ocean at night?" Chase sounded dazed.

"Quickest way to get across. I'll do it tomorrow night."

"What am I going to do?" he asked.

"You and I are going to rest here, and then you'll go back on one of the ferries tomorrow with the tourists."

"I might need something better than this," he pulled his grimy, bloody tee shirt away from him.

"Let's look in the vans, see if we can find you a jacket or something."

A search of both vans yielded not only a jacket in the ugliest plaid I'd ever seen, and I'm Scottish, but another tee shirt and two blankets.

"Let's go into one of the buildings," I said.

Chase followed me as I led him to one of the ruins, although not where the snipers had been killed.

I laid out the blankets while he changed his tee shirt. "You'll need to take that with you," I said, pointing to the bloodied one. "We don't want to leave your blood here."

He shoved it into the jacket pocket.

As we sat down, and then laid on the less than comfortable ground, Chase sighed. "I don't think I've ever been so tired."

He opened an arm toward me, giving me the choice.

I slid close to him, resting my head on his chest, even though the smell of his blood was intoxicating. I needed to distract myself. "Are you too tired to talk?" I asked.

CHAPTER SIXTEEN

Chase

I lay very still. "What do you want to talk about?" I asked.

She sighed against my chest. "About us."

"Why did you come for me?"

Morag turned her head to look up at me. "I wasn't sure it was you. I woke up, feeling like something had gone very wrong, and then Lyall—he's like our psychic, don't ask, it's too long of a story right now—he said that he felt it too. He could tell that something had gone badly somewhere around the island, and we went looking for it. I hoped it was you, so I could see you again. But I didn't want it to be you, because I didn't want to think of you hurting."

"This has really been my week for getting my ass

kicked," I said wryly. "Not exactly a great way to show you my best side."

"Are you kidding?" She asked.

"Sort of. Not really," I said.

"Don't be a dumb ass. You've been incredibly brave."

"And yet, I still stood by while people died."

"You did. But you did something else, too. You refused to go after the women. After the children," Morag said.

"It's not enough."

"Let's table that for a moment," she said. "I need to talk about us. I've felt horrible since you left."

"Hey," I held up a hand. "Let's set the record straight. You sent me away."

"Why did you go back to your family?"

I'd been asking myself that very thing ever since I woke up hog-tied in the back of a van. "I wanted to do things right. I wanted to tell them I was leaving. I wanted to say good bye to my mom."

"Where is your mom?" She looked up at me again.

"I don't know. She didn't say a word when my dad and brothers beat me senseless, or when they tossed me in a van and drove away, planning to do who knows what. She had to have known."

"Do you want to go and find her?"

"No," I said. "No. She left me to whatever Dad had planned. I hope she gets away and tries to live a better life. But I don't want to see her."

I'm an orphan, I thought. I have no one. And... I

didn't know how to feel about it. I knew that I'd struggle with this. But...

"You still have me," Morag said, interrupting my thoughts.

"How did you—"

"I could feel your sense of loss." She laid her head on my chest again.

"Do I have you?" I asked. "You didn't want me."

"Nothing could be further from the truth. I want you. I want you with every fiber of my being. My whole body ached after you left. I've been miserable. I couldn't live without you, feeling your heart, not being with you."

"So what are you saying?" I asked, hardly daring to hope.

She took a breath. But she didn't look at me. "I was going to die," she said softly.

"What?" I asked. I struggled to sit up, pulling her with me. "What are you talking about?"

"I realized I couldn't live like this for the rest of your life. So I was going to go away and meet the sun."

"Why would you do that?"

"I can feel your heartbeat, no matter how far away you've been from me. All I want is to be with you. I couldn't have you, so I thought. I couldn't live feeling you like that. And if you'd found a wife..." her voice trailed off.

"There is no one for me now that I've met you," I said, turning her face so I could kiss her.

"Oh, what, you love me now?"

"No, but I might," I said with a smile. I winced as she leaned into me.

"Oh, good hell, I forgot you're a mess," Morag said.

"Thanks for that. I feel so much better," I said.

"I can help you," she said.

"How?"

"I can give you my blood. We heal quickly. It can help you heal."

"How do I get this miracle cure?" I asked.

"I'll bite my wrist, and—"

"How about I bite you?" I asked.

Morag inhaled. "Dear God, I don't know if I could stand it."

"What, it's nice?" I asked.

Her eyes closed. "You have no idea."

A jealous haze clouded my vision at the thought of someone else tasting Morag's blood.

"Calm down," she said.

"All right," I said. "Will it turn me?" I didn't know how I felt about being turned, and I sure as hell didn't want to fight with her about it now.

"No. You'd need to lose nearly all your blood and take a lot more of mine. You don't have to do this," she said.

"No, I need to heal so I don't bring down the police when I get the hell off this godforsaken island."

"It's actually a shrine to God," Morag said primly.

"Shut up," I said. "Tell me what needs to happen."

"Okay, then. Let me—" I stopped her as she made to do something. I didn't know what she had in mind, but I suddenly knew what I wanted.

I stood up, pulling her with me and stripped off her pants. Then I let my jeans fall to the ground. Carefully, aware that I might start bleeding if I bumped something too hard, I sat down, and carefully pulled her into my lap facing me. "Oh, shit," I said, as Morag nestled into my lap, making my cock as hard as it had ever been.

"What? Are you all right?" She peered at me, looking for the injury causing my distress.

"I don't have anything, no protection," I said.

Morag looked at me, her face blank, and then laughed. "Oh, don't worry about it."

"But—"

"It's really tough for us to conceive. It happens, but not like it does for humans."

"You sure?" I asked.

She nodded and stood up so that she could lower herself onto my cock.

Carefully, slowly, with incredible tenderness, Morag moved on me. She was precise in where she put her hands—it was what I needed.

"I want to bite you," I said. I didn't know if this was the right time, but given her expression when she'd talked about it, I figured it was no great leap that biting and sex went hand in hand.

Just because I kept getting my ass kicked didn't mean I was stupid.

"Can I, would you let me," her voice was breathy.

I knew what she wanted. I stopped her. "Yes," I said.

"You first," she said. "Here. Bite hard, harder than you think you need to. The skin is tough." She leaned her neck to the side, patting the soft spot above the collarbone.

I kissed her neck, and found that when faced with it, I was a little nervous. I licked my lips, and then bit down harder than I'd ever bitten anything.

Her blood rushing into my mouth, and it was like an electric shock went through my entire body. I jumped as I felt a piercing pain in my own neck and realized she'd bit me right after I'd bit her. I could feel her sucking, and it made me suck her neck harder.

There was no way to describe it. It was like an orgasm on multiple levels. I felt it in every cell, every pore of my body. I thrust up into her as she pressed her body against me, feeling myself come in what felt like a shower of stars.

Then her mouth moved off me, and she pulled my head from her neck. "I love feeling you drink from me, but it's hard to stop," she kissed me, our mouths red with the blood of one another.

"That was," I said, as we sat, still joined, my heart thundering, covered in sweat even in the cool of the night. Well, I was sweating. Morag was as cool as ever.

"Amazing," she finished. "We have to work this out, Chase. I can't live without you."

"What, you love me now?"

"I like your body," she said.

"Good to know I'll be objectified properly."

We both laughed.

"I mean it," Morag said. "If my coven can't accept you, we'll leave."

"We could leave now," I said.

"No," she said, running her hands through my hair. "That's not the way to do this."

"So what do we do?"

"Take the ferry over. Start walking north. When a car comes by, ask for a lift to Lochdon House. They'll take you. The people who watch it during the day, Martin and Constance, they'll be awake and there. I'll meet you tomorrow night." Morag's nose wrinkled. It was probably the most adorable thing I'd ever seen. "I need to shower, to get the smell out. I already smell like a fish market."

"You smell delicious," I said, kissing her head. "You're sure about this?"

"Aren't you?"

"Yes," I said.

We lay twined together, and I fell asleep with her in my arms. Where she was supposed to be.

When I woke, it was just before sunrise. Morag was gone, and all my clothes were set out on the blanket. I got up, dressed, and went down toward the cliffs, to sit in the rocks where I wouldn't be as visible as the tourists started to arrive.

I fell asleep again, and when I opened my eyes, the sun was high in the sky. I got up, feeling like death on a stick, and tried to tidy myself. I noted that my wounds were healed, even as I wasn't feeling in top shape yet. I still looked like I'd had the shit kicked out of me many times. It was pretty much a lost cause, but I buttoned up the jacket, and headed for the ferry dock, hoping for the best.

Putting my hands in my pockets, I found there was a wad of money. When I got to the dock, I pleaded a lost ticket, and was able to buy my way back on.

Once on Mull, I started walking. Soon enough, a car came by and I was able to get a ride to Lochdon House. The man, named Jacob, told me to tell Collum, Martin, and Constance hello before he motored back down the drive.

The door opened before I had a chance to knock, and a short, grandmotherly woman opened the door.

"Saint's above," she said. "You must be Chase."

I nodded.

"We've been expecting you. Collum did say you'd be all in. He might not have spoken strongly enough," she said, looking me over.

"It's been a rough couple of days," I said.

"It usually is. Well, come in. I'm Constance, the housekeeper. Let's get some food into you, and then off to a shower and bed."

I let her direct me, and when she showed me to a room, it was all I could do to haul myself into the shower. My wounds had healed, but I was tired, more tired than I'd ever been in my life.

The one good thing, besides being clean, was that soon I'd see Morag.

I closed my eyes, a smile on my face. Soon.

CHAPTER SEVENTEEN

Morag

*a*s was usual since I'd met Chase, I hadn't slept deeply. His heartbeat and mine wouldn't let me. But today, I was happy about it. He was alive. And we were going to be together. I'd never felt happier in my entire life.

All that I needed to know now was where we'd end up. I meant what I said—if the coven said they didn't want him there, and it was a legitimate concern about what they would decide at this point, we'd leave. I loved my coven, but I could not and would not abandon my mate. Not ever again.

When it was dark, I ran across the abbey grounds, and into the water. I didn't care that it was cold, or that it smelled fishier than ever. I wanted to get home and see Chase.

As I ran up the hill to the house, I raced in the door and right to my room. I took a longer than normal shower—I wasn't going to smell like the sea again—and then went down to the dining room.

Every member of my coven was there. They were waiting.

"You look better," Collum said.

"Smell better too," Margaret said, arms crossed as she leaned against Devon. He smiled, putting an arm around her waist.

"Yes, I do. Where is Chase?"

"He's not up yet," Clara, Lyall's mate said with a smile. "He's been sleeping all day."

"Is he all right?" I asked, looking around wildly. No one had checked on him? I listened to my heart, and the beat was steady and relaxed. He was still sleeping peacefully.

"Is he?" Angus, sitting next to his mate Kyla, asked.

"He is," I said, a smile I couldn't stop creeping over my face.

"We'll save the discussion for when he wakes." Collum was firm. "So go do something else until he wakes. He may have had your blood, but he's still human."

"Like what?" I threw up my hands, frustrated.

"Go to the pubs. See if they're talking about the vans, or the bodies," Talbot suggested.

"Call me the minute he wakes," I said, giving everyone the evil eye.

"Oh, aren't we all protective?" Margaret asked the room at large.

Everyone met the eyes of everyone else. Normally, teasing me like that would bring a laugh, smiles at the least. But they hadn't even smiled. Shit. They were going to tell me he had to leave.

My anxiety spiked. I couldn't stop it.

"Go," Collum said. "I can't stand all the energy rolling off you."

"Fine. I'm gone," I said.

I wanted nothing more than to be with Chase, but I knew he was sleeping to heal. I wanted nothing more than to put it all on the table and get the discussions over with. But it needed to wait. Chase deserved to hear it just as I did.

The isle was abuzz with the vans that had been found. One of the bodies had washed up on Mull–the common believe was that they'd gone out to Iona up to no good, drinking and carrying on, and had fallen off the cliffs. That, at least, was a relief. When I went home about an hour before sunrise, Collum was sitting with Isabeau in the front room.

"He hasn't woken. I think he might sleep through tomorrow."

"Damn it," I said.

"I know you're wanting to get this over with, but everyone needs to be there."

I sighed, feeling very aggrieved. "All right. I'm going to bed."

They both nodded, not saying anything else.

Shit. They'd already decided. Why else would everyone be so solemn?

Well, I couldn't do anything about it until tomorrow. Might as well sleep. I fell into my restless sleep, comforted by the heartbeat in the room next to me.

The heartbeat of my mate. Who would be with me from this point on, regardless of what happened tomorrow.

With that thought, I let my body relax. Tomorrow would be here soon enough.

CHAPTER EIGHTEEN

Chase

*T*he sun on my face woke me. I stretched in bed, feeling... pretty good. I'd been dog tired when I came to bed last night and now, I felt good.

Far better than I should given the number of ass kickings I'd sustained this week. Morag's blood was like a super vitamin that healed. I rubbed the spot where she'd bitten me, and there was nothing there.

"Whoa," I said out loud. I got out of bed, needing to see it for myself. I looked at myself in the mirror in the bathroom—nothing.

Lifting up my shirt—my bruises were gone as though they'd never been there, and I felt like I'd only been beaten up once. This shit was amazing.

I took a shower, letting the water run nearly cold. Was I a horrible human? A horrible brother and son? I didn't feel all that bad that my family was gone, most of them dead. Not only would they have killed me, but they would have tried to kill Morag. All the vampires here.

I recalled the conversation at the abbey. Morag had meant to die. I needed to make her see that was never an option, to make her promise she'd never take that option.

Worst-case scenario, Morag and I would be on our own. For her sake, I hoped it wouldn't come to that, but I honestly thought she was being optimistic to think there was any other resolution.

I went downstairs, following the smells. Constance was in the kitchen, and she made me a sandwich, and soup, and would have offered more if I could have stood it.

"They'll be up right at sunset, dearie," she said. "You're welcome around the main floor. Collum asked that you stay inside and don't go wandering upstairs. That's where their rooms are, you know. It's good to see you up, you having slept through the day yesterday."

"What?" I asked.

"You didn't wake up last night. You slept all day, and through the night. It's late afternoon, now. I know Morag has been worried," she smiled at me, showing her dimples.

"How long have you worked for them?" I asked. I'd never met anyone who worked for vampires.

"Oh," she looked away, thinking. "Fourteen years

now? My husband, Martin, is the caretaker around the grounds, while I take care of the house, and we keep things going for them during the day. They're kind and take good care of us."

"Where do you live?" I asked.

"We have a little house a bit that way," she lifted a hand, gesturing to the front of the house. "Down the drive. Collum said it's ours forever. No matter if we work for them or not."

"You don't mind working for vampires?"

She looked surprised. "No, why would I? They don't go around biting people, they're kind, polite, they're good to the island and the people here—what's to mind?"

What indeed? I nodded, and thanked her for lunch, deciding I'd sit in the library.

Which is where Collum found me several hours later. "Morag is almost down. She'll be in in a moment. Then I'm asking you to join us for a discussion in the dining room." His face was neutral.

"All right," I said.

"That's done, then," he said, and walked back out.

A few moments later, Morag came in. She flew into my arms, and I wrapped them around her, breathing in the scent of her hair, loving the feel of her cool body next to mine.

"You're better?" she asked, looking up at me.

"I am. Whatever's in your blood, it's great. I feel amazing."

She smiled. "Then let's go meet them."

"Together," I said.

"Together," she replied.

Hand in hand, we walked into the dining room. There were ten vampires there, five men and five women. I recognized a few from the night on Iona.

Collum sat in the middle of the table and there were two chairs across from him that were empty. "Sit down, and stop looking like you're coming to the firing squad," he said irritably.

"Aren't we?" I asked.

"Do you deserve to be?" Collum didn't beat around the bush.

"I do," I said. "Morag doesn't."

"That's true," another man said. He'd been on Iona as well. He was the fiercer of the two other men who'd been there.

"Why did you abandon your family?" Collum asked.

Whatever I'd been expecting, that wasn't it. I took a moment before replying. I was still alive, and they seemed to value honesty, even if it wasn't what they wanted to hear.

So I gave them honesty. I told them about how I'd grown to doubt what my family had termed as a calling. How the events of last week had pushed me over the edge, and why I'd ended up in Edinburgh.

"You left Morag before," a young woman sitting next to Collum, who looked to be my age—although none of them looked old—said to me. "Why?"

"Morag told me she didn't want to see me anymore," I said. "I don't force women."

There was a silence around the table. Collum looked around.

The woman who'd been holding my dad and who had killed him, spoke up. She was a tall, thin woman, with a firm mouth and no nonsense eyes. Her name was Margaret, if I was remembering right. "I'll open the dance. I vote yes."

"Why?" Collum asked. There was murmuring around the table.

"He fucked up. He lived the life of a killer. So do we," she shrugged. "We've learned how to be better. When I was turned, people died so I could eat. Now, there are better ways. If we can learn, so can a Hunter. And frankly, it takes some guts to stand and watch your family die, particularly when they died because you said they should. It seems to me Chase has chosen a side and pledged himself and his loyalty pretty thoroughly." She nodded, as if that answered the question.

One of the other men, whose name I didn't know, said, "You think that's enough? For all the lives he took?"

"What kind of death is worse, Angus?" Margaret asked him.

"What do you mean?" Angus asked.

"Is it worse to know someone died, or someone you know died?"

"Well, of course someone you know," Angus said.

135

He was wary, not sure where Margaret was heading with this.

"Chase," she gestured at me, "watched us wrench the necks of his father and brothers. Now they were pathetic hulks of humans and complete wastes, but they *were* his family. And he watched them die. He told us they had to die. So in my humble opinion," Margaret leaned back, "He's made payment."

"He didn't betray us," Morag said.

"That's true," the fierce man who'd agreed with Collum said. Talbot? Was that his name?

The other man whose name I remembered, Lyall, nodded. "It is. They told him they'd go easy on him if he told them where to find us. He told them to fuck off."

"Well said," Margaret said, meeting my eyes. "Go out with defiance."

I wanted to smile, but I only nodded.

"I vote yes," the woman sitting next to Collum said. "We all make mistakes. I nearly killed Collum," she shrugged. "It wasn't deliberate. Chase tried to protect Morag and protect all of us because of her."

"You didn't nearly kill me," Collum said, rolling his eyes.

There was something that passed around the table, some level of communication I couldn't decipher. Morag took my hand under the table. I had no idea whether that meant we were doing well, or if it was all about to go to shit.

"We're decided?" Collum asked, looking around.

They all nodded.

He looked at me. "You are welcome to stay here, Chase Robson, mate of Morag MacLean. But you will swear an oath to me, on the pain of death for both of you, that you will renounce all your loyalty to your former family. That you will let us know should any of them come here, or threaten us in any way. Will you give me your oath to do this, to swear allegiance to this clan?"

"I will," I said.

"We have all witnessed," Collum said formally. Welcome to the Clan MacLean," he added as he stood up. "There will be more for you to do and learn, but there's time. Now, I think that it's time we gave the newest couple some privacy. Morag, you'll let me know?"

Morag nodded.

There were smiles, the first I'd seen since Morag and I walked in, and everyone left.

"I feel like I just went through some kind of test," I said. "And I'm not sure if I passed it."

She smiled at me in a way that was like seeing the sun come out. "You passed. We all decide whether to add new members to our coven. Especially when there is something to be concerned about. And they all agreed."

"Why?" I asked. I wasn't looking the gift horse in the mouth, but I was really surprised. "And what do you need to let Collum know?"

"I think Margaret tipped it. Next to me, she's the fiercest fighter. As for Collum's request, we can talk about that later."

"You're the fiercest?" I asked.

She nodded, without any false pride. "I like to fight. I like to take out our enemies. I love my family."

I grinned. "Fate matched us well."

"What, you love me now?" Morag asked.

"No, but I might. You keep gaining points." I reached for her, pulling her into my lap.

"I could think of some things that might gain me more," she said, her lips curving into a wicked smile.

"Oh, really? I'm pretty demanding," I said.

"Maybe now that you're healed," she laughed.

"Oh, you will pay for that," I growled, kissing the back of her neck.

"Please, please make me pay," Morag slid off my lap, leading me away.

She ran out the door, and called, "Come on, slowpoke!"

I ran after her. This was the hunt I was made for.

EPILOGUE

Morag
The Following Year
A Summer Evening

I fussed with my dress, twitching it this way and that way. I was more comfortable in soft, stretchy pants and boots. But here I was, trussed like a chicken headed for the table.

"Stop," Kyla said. "It'll be over soon enough."

"So you say," I grumbled.

There was a hum in the air, a buzz of conversation. A great many of the islanders had been invited, and they all had showed. We didn't invite company often. I'd told Collum this was going to be a cluster, but he'd insisted. I was the last one to find my mate, and he said I needed to do this for all of us.

"Are you ready?" Isabeau stuck her head in.

"She is," Clara said, her smile broad. "Come on, Morag, no sense in delaying."

Together with Kyla and Clara, I walked from my room down the stairs. Charlotte and Margaret were in charge of getting the guests out onto the lawn, under the canopy we'd put up just for today.

I stopped at the door. My coven, save Collum, stood around me.

"Can't believe this is here," Angus said.

"He's some kind of saint, to put up with her humors," Talbot teased.

"Stop it, you two," Charlotte shushed them. "Morag, you look gorgeous."

"Like our opinion matters," Devon said with a smile.

"You still want do it like this?" Isabeau asked.

I nodded. There was no other way I'd want to do this.

"Well, all right."

Margaret gave me a one-armed hug as she walked by with Devon.

My coven mates walked out before me, walking together with their respective mates, and I followed walking with Isabeau. I wanted no one but my family around me when I made my promise to my mate.

The music began as we walked down the aisle. Isabeau's parents and grandmother were in the front row, and Gran smiled as if I were her own. I could see Collum standing at the end, and then I got my first glimpse of Chase. He turned, and the sight of him in a tuxedo made my lust go into overdrive.

"Easy," Isabeau said.

That was bad if she could tell. I'd have to tone it down to get through the reception.

As I reached the spot where Chase waited for me, I heard Collum start to speak. Whatever he said, I couldn't tell. I was lost in Chase's eyes.

A year with him had made me see that fate chose exactly right for us both. We fit together. He and I trained together, and he ran patrols with me at night. He liked to be outside and doing something just as I did.

Chase had been at the castle for a week when he stopped while we were on a run, and made me swear to him I'd never consider dying again like I had before we'd made the choice to be together.

"I can't live with the thought that you'd ever see that as a solution," Chase said. "Promise me, Morag."

I'd promised. I was relieved it hadn't come to that. Since his heartbeat was right next to me every night, I wasn't on the verge of madness like I'd been before.

But the thought of losing him was always there. He was so human. Even as strong as he was, he was human.

There were times he woke up, racked with guilt— over the vampires he'd helped to give the final death, over his family—and I had to help him to work through it.

It was still a work in process for him. But what

helped him most, oddly enough, was the rest of our coven.

He told me once, which I promptly told the rest of the coven, that he felt he fit in better here after only a couple of months than he ever had with his human family. He also said, which I didn't repeat, that he felt the reason he went through what he did with that family was so that he could find me. So that I could find him. Because we were meant for each other. I'd almost cried when he said all the things he did—we'd come together in such a difficult manner. I wondered at times if he thought the loss was too great.

To know that he felt we were supposed to be together despite everything warmed me down to my toes.

With my concerns over his human state, I'd asked him if he wanted me to turn him. He'd thought it over for a day, taking longer than I thought he should have. I was getting ready to be really offended when he came to me with an answer.

"I'm loving being with you just like this," he said. "Can we go on like this a little longer? I promise, I won't delay forever."

And he'd sweetened his request with some seriously hot sex. What could I do but say okay? He'd asked me to marry him four months ago. I told him it wasn't necessary, but he said he really wanted this with me. So I said yes.

To my surprise, the rest of the coven was extremely enthusiastic about a wedding.

Which was why I was here now, in front of most of the Isle of Mull, dolled up like I'd never been before. But Chase was here with me, holding my hands, and that made it all worthwhile.

"I do," I said when he squeezed my hands to bring me back into the moment.

"I do," Chase said a moment later. His eyes met mine. There was no one else but us.

Then he was leaning close to kiss me, and right before our lips met, he whispered, "So what? You love me now?"

"You'd better believe it," I whispered against his lips. "You're mine." We kissed, our first kiss as husband and wife.

Chase wrapped an arm around my waist, dipping me down so that our faces were away from the people watching. "I love you, too," he whispered.

"I love you forever," I kissed him hungrily.

As his fangs nipped at my bottom lip, drawing blood, he licked my lips and then stood back up. "We have forever," he said.

"Yes, we do."

We clasped hands and turned to face our future together. We might be in eternal, immortal darkness, but we were in it together, and that meant everything was right.

~

Love reading about the Clan MacLean? Dive into
Collum and Isabeau's story in
FOREVER BLOOD.
And stay tuned to The Midnight Coven's latest doings
in our Facebook group.
We've got lots more planned for you!
Keep reading for the next book in the Vampire Mates
series, IMMORTAL OATH,
by Corinne O'Flynn. The first chapter is next!

IMMORTAL OATH

Chapter One
HARRY

I've always found gambling on cards thrilling, but it's the study of the people playing with me that keeps it from becoming monotonous and boring. Indeed, after two hundred forty years on this earth, people are the only things keeping immortality interesting.

The Texas Hold'em dealer lays three cards on the table for all of us to see. The guy across from me eyes the community cards we all share and fiddles with one of the dials on his elaborate wristwatch—that's his tell; he likes the hand he's been dealt.

The woman next to him freezes her face in a blank expression as if she's playing a children's game of statues, she so deliberate about it I almost want to tell her. This is what she does when she, too, likes her hand.

I don't have to turn my head to know the young man seated to my right is happy with his cards; there are still two more cards to come and I can already hear his heart racing as he contemplates his wager.

I have the ace and king of diamonds in my hand. On the table lay the king of hearts, the queen of diamonds, and the ten of diamonds. Could be a Royal Flush for me, if lady luck is smiling tonight, or it could be a Straight Flush, ace high. Or, it could be a measly pair of kings, in which case I should probably cash in my chips and call it a night, as the losing streak I am on is starting to hurt my feelings.

But where is the fun in that?

"Five hundred." I lift five one-hundred dollar chips from my smallest stack and toss them into the pot. It's the minimum bid at this table and nobody bats an eyelash. My mind wanders as the other players contemplate their bets. Our dealer watches and waits with indifference, or perhaps she's wearing a mask as well. I don't spend much time studying the dealers, they are already being watched by the eyes in the sky. Nothing they do can influence the outcome here without causing some serious consequences for them.

My attention shifts as a door opens at the back of the long room and five men and one woman emerge. They stand together as the door swings shut behind them and they scan the crowded casino with a practiced gaze. They're gauging the people in the room, looking for danger.

Well, hello there. I feel a smile quirk up the corner of my mouth. I've been curious to get a look at the elusive local vampires in Las Vegas since Miles and Delilah and I arrived in the early hours last night. Miles said he'd cleared our little visit with Sorin Ludovici, the coven leader here, but none of them cared for a face-to-face to make our greetings and shake hands.

Miles relayed their conversation from yesterday. Sorin made it clear that I would be tolerated, and nothing more. He wasn't impressed that I came here under the protection of Collum. "I don't care if Lucifer himself sent him to you for safekeeping. He's on the run from every hunter group there is. We don't need that sort of trouble here. So, have your fun and go back to Lake Tahoe where you belong."

Miles seemed unfazed by the brushoff. I suppose after what I've done, I can't blame anyone for wanting me gone. One cannot expect to kill and dismember twenty-seven hunters in one night, flinging their bloody body parts all over the house, leaving them to rot, and expect everyone to understand.

Whatever. I restrain myself out of respect for Miles and Delilah. I am here as their guest and I wouldn't want to disrupt any relationships he's forged over the years with the Vegas vampires. But should things change, I am ruled by no one. I go where I please.

Delilah wrinkled her nose as Miles shared the warning from Sorin. "He sounds like a real sour puss."

Miles shrugged. "Harry did make quite a stir before leaving Scotland, my love." He wrapped his arm around her and pulled her to him, smiling as he nuzzled her neck. "He's an unknown quantity as far as they're concerned. Give it time. Once they get to know him..."

"Quite a stir?" Delilah repeated, scoffing.

I laughed. "That's one way of putting it, Miles."

Back in Scotland, when my coven was attacked, the hunters responsible made a point of torturing every one of my family before they killed them.

It wasn't enough that they found our sleeping place. It wasn't enough that they could prey upon fifteen sleeping vampires and stake them without a fuss. No, they saw fit to wrap my family in silver wire and then whip them with silver-tipped lashes, burning and disfiguring each of them in turn while the others watched.

They treated the women like animals. They tortured the children—*children*! Not satisfied enough to just kill them, the hunters dragged my family outside and forced them to meet the sun.

I'd been away for a fortnight. I returned in time to see the end of the carnage. The sun was about to rise, or I would have intervened. Instead, I had no choice but to dig myself a deep hole and hide in the dirt while my family turned to ash.

As the sun broke over the horizon, they all screamed for our mother.

"Fenella! Fenella!" They wept and tried to say their goodbyes in the moments they had left.

Fenella did not cry. She sensed that I was near and turned my way, her silver blond hair hanging long down her back, still striking and beautiful despite the blood and skin clumping in her locks. Her final thoughts were seared into my mind.

Kill them all, Harry. Every last one. Avenge us.

And that's exactly what I did, and I didn't care about leaving a mess.

As soon as the sun sank below the horizon, I burst from the earth and scented the hunters, tracking them back to their lair. They were celebrating together, all in one place, the fools.

They did not die quickly. I tore all of them apart— literally limb from limb. Their screams did nothing to assuage my wrath, but I did not stop until I had destroyed all of them.

But a few of them apparently got away, and now my scruffy mug sits at the top of their Most Wanted list.

To which I say, bring it—I've got nothing else to lose.

The dealer flips over the next card for the table and my attention is back on the game. If I needed my lungs to breathe, I may have gasped. The two of diamonds winks at me as if daring me to go all-in. Worst case I am flush with diamonds, and there's still one card to go. I think about it and wonder if perhaps luck is with me tonight.

"There you go, darling." The waitress places my whiskey on the table next to me.

I inhale, filling my lungs so I may say thank you when the scent of her overtakes me. I turn to look at her and have to clamp my mouth shut as my fangs descend.

Her olive skin glows in the warm light of the chandeliers. A wall sconce behind us illuminates her eyes, which are bright green and absolutely fierce. Her dark brown hair hangs over her shoulder in a long braid. I have to look up at her from my low chair and when her green eyes meet mine, I watch her pupils dilate as she takes me in.

"Hello, love," I say, my voice low. It's all I can manage—all I can think to say. My brain is no longer sending signals to my mouth. I move my gaze over her slim frame, admiring the way her collar bone peeks out of her blouse, her shapely breasts, her lovely bottom, the taut energy of her. When I bring my eyes back to her face, she's watching me.

She arches a brow as if to say, *really*? "Simmer down, Tiger." Her voice is deep and there's an edge to it that tells me she can and will stand on her own.

I hear her words but they don't match what's going on with her eyes and her pulse. When she meets my gaze, it's like time pauses for a long moment to allow us the space to really see. She bites her lower lip as I run my tongue over my fangs, still hidden by my closed mouth.

"Sir?" a voice calls from outer space.

She touches my shoulder and tips her chin at the dealer. "You're up."

I turn to look at her hand resting on me. Her slender fingers end in neatly manicured nails, her polish a pale pink. Then I watch her walk away, her drink tray in one hand, her muscular body moving through the tables like a cat.

"Sir," the dealer says.

I turn back to the game and feel like I've been gone for an hour. I draw my fangs back and lick my lips. "Sorry. Forgive me."

"The bet is five thousand to you."

I finger the stacks of chips before me as I gauge the other players. Wristwatch spins, Statue is still, and the heartbeat next to me is so loud it's a wonder everyone isn't taking note. I count off five thousand and raise another five, bringing the ante to ten thousand for anyone who wishes to stay in the game and see that last card dealt.

The dealer takes my chip stacks and lays them out for the cameras and calls a manager over to verify before pulling it into the pot. Wristwatch groans as he adds his chips. Statue doesn't make a sound as her bet is added as well. They both eye me furtively and then watch the cards. Heartbeat guy folds, unwilling to cover the bet. He tosses a hundred to the dealer, thanks the table, and pushes off with a sigh of frustration as he shakes his head and leaves the room.

But the racing heart in my ears does not lessen. It does not fade away as the distance between us grows. The heartbeat in my ears remains steady and strong. This isn't right. I can usually control my ability to connect and listen to others... why can't I stop hearing his heart?

I look down at my hand, which rests on the table next to my cards. The light seems to move over my skin in concert with the sound. My vampire vision is acute, and my ability to see details a human couldn't possibly notice seems to be tricking me. I watch as the veins visible in my hands twitch in time to the heart beat ringing through my ears.

The dealer flips the final card onto the table. The Jack of diamonds stares back at me with his two beady eyes. Wristwatch actually gasps. The crowd which has gathered around the table to watch the high rollers reveal their hands, lets out a collective *oooh!*

I place my hand over my heart and feel a pulse beat, beat, beating under my cold flesh.

"Reveal your cards please, sir." The dealer's voice is drowned out by the pulse raging in my ears. She nods at me and then looks pointedly at my cards, which lay face down on the red felt table.

I realize the room is watching me. I must compose myself.

My heart, which hasn't stirred since I was made in the year 1805, is beating.

I turn my cards over on the table to reveal my Royal Flush as the crowd explodes in cheers of excitement and joy. Hands clap me on the back and perfumed women kiss my cheeks. They all want to be near the big winner.

"Are you all right? Should I call for assistance?" The dealer watches me as I clutch my chest.

I've just won over a hundred thousand dollars on a single hand. I have to laugh because the humans around me think I am clutching my heart for the shock of the windfall. If only they knew that the money meant little to me; I had wealth to last several lifetimes. No, I couldn't relish the victory because my entire focus was consumed by my beating heart.

I know what it means. I've heard many vampires talk about their hearts waking after lifetimes of stillness once they had met their mates. In my short time since arriving in Lake Tahoe, Miles already told me the story of how Delilah had done this very thing to him.

"Astounding." My words disappear into the din of celebration around me.

My mate is here. But whom?

I glance around the room, but between the crowd encircling me and the casino manager standing next to the dealer, my view is reduced to a narrow sliver of space.

And that's when I see her.

The cocktail waitress who called me Tiger and told me to simmer down. The one who touched my shoulder and made time seem to slow.

She walks by the pack of vampires at the back of the room. The female vamp steps in front of the men, blocking her path, and forcing the waitress to stop.

I feel my heart race a little—it's like a quick zing of fear—and realize with a start that my heart isn't just beating, it's beating in time with hers.

She lifts her chin and stares at one of the vampires, challenging him. He smiles at her, but it's condescending. Then he bends to whisper something into her ear. Her heartbeat—my heartbeat—slows to a languid, easy rhythm as her shoulders relax.

The female vamp takes the drink tray and places it on a table as the vampires lead the waitress back to the door.

The last thing I see before the door closes is the dopey smile on the waitress' face. It is the unmistakable grin of someone who has been glamoured.

**You've just read Chapter One of IMMORTAL OATH by Corinne O'Flynn.
You can find more of this story here:**
https://books2read.com/immortaloath

The Vampire Mates Series

Are you willing to taste immortality?
Come with us and let our vampires glamour you into a
world full of dangerous magic, toe-curling heat, and a
love to last forever.

The Vampire Mates series by the Midnight Coven

contains thirteen tales penned by your favorite best-selling paranormal romance authors.

Each novella can be read as a complete standalone, but of course, we hope you'll bite into them all.
With our Vampire Mates at your side, immortality is sexy AF.

- Immortal Hexes by Amelia Hutchins
https://books2read.com/u/mv2796

- Immortal Promise by Kim Loraine-Author
https://books2read.com/immortalpromise/

- Immortal Hunter by Patricia D. Eddy
https://books2read.com/u/mZNRE2

- Immortal Bite by Andrea M. Long
https://books2read.com/u/bpKX8z

- Immortal Bloodlines by Jessica Cage
https://books2read.com/u/m2PO7R

- Immortal Night by Emily Goodwin

- Immortal Darkness by Lisa Manifold
https://books2read.com/Immortaldarkness

- Immortal Oath by Corinne O'Flynn

https://books2read.com/immortaloath

• Immortal Awakening by Renea Mason

• Immortal Devotion by Gwen Knight
https://books2read.com/immortaldevotion

• Immortal Enemies by Jessie Lane
https://books2read.com/immortalenemies

• Immortal Skye by KL Bone
https://books2read.com/Immortal-Skye

• Immortal Protector by Alice K. Wayne
https://books2read.com/u/3nKwrx

Before there were the Vampire Mates, there were the Vampire Brides.

Love never dies. But it can be damn bloody.

Forever Blood
Isabeau

Everyone I love is dead and buried, along with any hope I had for a happy life. I'm learning how to live again; I just didn't expect it to be so damned hard. Tired of my pity party, my grandmother sends me packing. Before I know it, I'm on the windy shores of Scotland with a map and a plan, courtesy of Gran.

When a mysterious guy crashes my sightseeing tour, I don't even know his name, but I feel like I'm tasting life for the first time in a year. I can't keep my eyes off him, and the feeling is clearly mutual. But when he reveals his true nature to me, I'm not as surprised by him as I am afraid of myself.

I've just learned to love life again; why in the world would I give that up for anyone?

Collum

I might be a predator, but I haven't killed in over two hundred years. Life is fragile, and even someone as powerful as I has learned the cost of a life taken. So when I meet Isabeau, I'm reminded of the promise I made with myself; a solemn pact drawn up after a tragic loss. There are many benefits to being immortal, living without a mate is not one of them.

I think I know the way this story is supposed to end and I'm surprised when Isabeau has other plans. She lights a fire in me I have not felt in an age but my past has taught me one thing.

Nothing is promised to the damned.

The Midnight Coven presents: Vampire Brides
Tall, dark and handsome, these vampires are no
strangers to the art of the hunt. Seduction and
secrecy have ruled their lives for centuries, but these
eleven alpha vamps are about to meet their matches
and say "I do" to their forever mates.

This is a stand-alone novella in the Vampire Brides series, a shared world of stories from eleven best-selling authors.

ABOUT THE AUTHOR

Lisa Manifold is a *USA Today* Bestselling Author of fantasy, paranormal, and romance stories. She moved to Colorado as an adult and has no plans of living anywhere else. She is a consummate reader, often running late because "Just one more page!" She is a fan of all things Con, and has an entire room devoted to the costumes created for Cons.

Lisa is the author of many flavors of paranormal series, including The Realm, Djinn Everlasting, Dragon Thief, The Aumahnee Prophecy, Tales from the Veil, Sisters of the Curse, the books from The Midnight Coven collective, the Deadwood Sisters and The Mostly Open Paranormal Investigative Agency.

She lives as close to the mountains as possible with her husband, children, and four red rescue dogs.

Stay in touch:
Sign up for my Newsletter and never miss a thing!
Website: www.lisamanifold.com
Or one of the links below.
Xoxo
Lisa

ALSO BY LISA MANIFOLD

Vampire Mates

(with The Midnight Coven)

Immortal Darkness

The Mostly Open Paranormal

Investigative Agency

Dark Pact

Dark Night (Oct 2019)

Vampire Brides

(with The Midnight Coven)

Forever Blood

Deadwood Sisters

Hellborn: The Unlucky Book 1

Hellfire: The Unlucky Book 2 (Sept 2019)

Dragon Thief

Dragon Lost

Dragon Found

The Realm Series

Heart of the Goblin King

To Wed the Goblin King

Realms of the Goblin King

Rise of the Dragon King

The Companion Tales, Volume I

The Companion Tales, Volume II

The Aumahnee Prophecy

with Corinne O'Flynn

Eamonn's Tale

Marigold's Tale

Watchers of the Veil

Defenders of the Realm

Tales From The Veil

with Corinne O'Flynn

The Portal Keepers

The Gimcrackers

Djinn Everlasting

Three Wishes

Forgotten Wishes

Hidden Wishes

Sisters of the Curse

Thea's Tale

One Night at the Ball

Casimir's Journey

Do you like being in the loop? Sign up for Lisa's newsletter! Shenanigans, book recs, and the latest news abound!

Want to see more of Lisa's books?

Visit www.Lisamanifold.com